Hidden Meanings . . .

"We can't be co-hosts," she blurted. "It'll never work."

"Why not?"

"You know as well as I do that you're on record as having ridiculed my fiancé and me—"

"That wasn't ridicule," he cut in. "It was an observation. No, that's not what's bothering you—not entirely."

Her breath caught as his blue eyes intensified in their scrutiny. He moved closer and took her arm. "You're afraid I'll see something you don't want seen, discover something you've neatly tucked away."

"Like what?"

His intimate inspection of her eyes, her mouth, her quickened breathing, brought an uncontrollable flush to her face; the warmth raced lower, down to her chest. His hand on her arm was their only physical connection, yet she felt threatened by him, invaded by him.

"A whole reservoir of feelings you haven't consciously acknowledged yet," he said, his voice oddly husky.

Dear Reader,

Welcome to Silhouette! Our goal is to give you hours of unbeatable reading pleasure, and we hope you'll enjoy each month's six new Silhouette Desires. These sensual, provocative love stories are both believable and compelling—sometimes they're poignant, sometimes humorous, but always enjoyable.

Indulge yourself. Experience all the passion and excitement of falling in love along with our heroine as she meets the irresistible man of her dreams and together they overcome all obstacles in the path to a happy ending.

If this is your first Desire, I hope it'll be the first of many. If you're already a Silhouette Desire reader, thanks for your support! Look for some of your favorite authors in the coming months: Stephanie James, Diana Palmer, Dixie Browning, Ann Major and Doreen Owens Malek, to name just a few.

Happy reading!

Isabel Swift
Senior Editor

SDRL-7/85

SUZANNE FORSTER
Hot
Properties

Silhouette Desire
Published by Silhouette Books New York
America's Publisher of Contemporary Romance

SILHOUETTE BOOKS
300 East 42nd St., New York, N.Y. 10017

ISBN: 0-373-05273-1

First Silhouette Books printing April 1986

America's Publisher of Contemporary Romance

Printed in the U.S.A.

SUZANNE FORSTER

started her writing career by accident—literally. She took up writing while confined to bed after a car accident, and her first published book was discovered quite accidentally by an editor who read it while judging the finalists in the 1984 Romance Writers of America writing contest. Accidents do happen, but Ms. Forster's talent is the real key to her success.

To my husband, Allan, for his unshakable
belief in the dream.

To my teacher, Pat Kubis, for her
ever-patient wisdom.

To my writing buddies—Linda, Millie,
Helen, Jack, Bob and Ann—for hanging
in there with me.

One

Chin up!'' Daphne ordered, whisking more Electric Coral blusher over Sunny Tyler's cheekbones. The elfin makeup artist stood, squinted at her work, then began scooping pencils, tubes and jars into her cosmetic case. ''Keep smiling,'' she muttered before disappearing through the dressing room door.

Sunny instinctively glanced back at the lighted makeup mirror, shook her shaggy, shoulder-length blond hair and tested her smile. The glass seemed to light up with her reflection. ''It still works,'' she said, exhaling gratefully. Sunny knew better than anyone that something magical happened to her rather ordinary face when she smiled. Her hazel eyes sparkled and her pleasing but too-round countenance took on a dazzling, life-is-terrific expression.

Silly as it seemed, she'd had nightmares about not being able to summon up that infectious smile when she needed it, nightmares about staring into the camera with a frozen, saucer-eyed Steve Martin gape. ''An unthinkable end to a promising career,'' she murmured. Soft laughter banished the thought but not the disturbing lightness in her stomach.

Pushing out of the makeup chair, she brushed hurriedly at the wrinkles in her silk shirtwaist. The *L.A. Examiner*, a pot of coffee and a plate of buttery brioche awaited her on the coffee table. She glanced at her watch—fifteen minutes to airtime—and picked up the paper. Fingers trembling a little, she sat down on the small rattan couch and leafed through to the People section.

What did the press have in store for her today? Would her name be splashed in the gossip columns again? Yesterday there'd been a rash of one-liners about her and Ted—that embarrassing "Ken and Barbie" business again—and even a few blasts at her interview show, *L.A. Heartbeat*. Her stomach did another tight flutter as she scanned the newsprint, searching.

There she was. Item two in Martha Benson's column:

> Could Sunny Tyler and her fiancé, junior congressman Ted Walsh, really be as boring as Graham Chance's recent interview with Ted made them out to be? 'Fraid so *Yawn.* Rumor has it that the congressman slipped into a coma during that interview and nobody knew! What's next? Ken and Barbie go to Washington?

Boring? Sunny crushed the paper as the dressing room door creaked open and a long face dwarfed by huge, horn-rimmed glasses peeked in. "Hello, beautiful!" the show's producer greeted her buoyantly. "You're looking especially fetching today."

With a muffled groan, she set aside the paper. Whenever Steve Freedkin plied her with compliments, she knew he'd just come up with some crazy new gimmick to boost ratings. "Morning, Steve," she said, inwardly fortifying herself. "Coffee?"

Shrugging off her offer, Steve shut the door and reached the coffee table with two loping strides. He should have been a basketball player, Sunny thought, her neck cricking as she stared up at the expressive face that topped his hyperactive, Olive Oyl body.

"Read this yet?" he asked, an odd look on his face as he held out a supermarket tabloid.

Her breath tightened expectantly. She shook her head, refusing to take the lurid gossip rag. She was determined not to let Steve or anyone else know how preoccupied she was with the recent glut of publicity.

He waved the paper temptingly. "You're not going to believe this, Sunny."

She eyed the tabloid, consumed with curiosity. Don't do it, Sunny, she warned, dignity prevailing... briefly. A frustrated sigh built. She leaned forward to take the paper, just as Steve absently flicked it back and opened it. "You made the 'Who's Feuding?' column," he announced, snorting. "Color pictures, bold print—everything, Sunny, the whole ball of wax!"

"Pictures, feuding?" she echoed darkly. "Ted and me?"

"No." He slapped the paper. "*You and Chance*—Graham Chance—the SOB whose talk show is systematically stealing away our viewers." He dropped the open tabloid in her lap.

Sunny stared down at the color photograph of the man whose recent careless comments had brought her such grief. Her blinking eyes took in his thick chestnut-gold hair, sunlightened eyebrows and striking blue eyes. Humor, intelligence—and something that might be mistaken for sincerity—positively shone from those eyes. Sunny knew better. Graham Chance was a blatant opportunist. And despite the perpetually cheerful disposition for which Sunny was named, she disliked this blue-eyed menace with mega-watt intensity.

Yet something, call it foolish pride, made her stubbornly resolve not to let anyone—and especially Graham Chance—know just how thoroughly he'd upset her life. "Nice picture," she said, clearing her throat as she closed the paper and handed it back to her producer. "But I've never met the man, so I can hardly be feuding with him, can I?" A glance at Freedkin told her he wasn't buying her sangfroid.

"Sunny," he said reprovingly, "tens of millions of Americans read this rag. They already know that Chance interviewed your fiancé last week and implied that the two of you were too good to be true. 'Squeaky clean,' I believe he said, and then there was that offhand remark about 'anatomically correct' Ken and Barbie dolls..."

As Freedkin went on, Sunny felt her exasperation build. She and Ted had been the butt of nonstop jokes ever since that godforsaken interview. Even Ted's fellow congressmen had taken to calling him "Kenikins," and Sunny's fans now yelled "yoo-hoo, Barbie." Pranksters left off-color Barbie remarks on her answering machine.

"That Chance is an artist, isn't he?" Freedkin continued, chuckling. "He sure had old Ted going...."

Sunny's neck muscles tensed. She found *nothing* funny in the situation. She'd even warned Ted before the interview, cautioned him that Graham Chance specialized in cutting through his guests' celebrity images. A former radio psychologist, Chance used confrontational interview techniques that elicited honest answers. Oh yes, Sunny admitted silently, Graham Chance was an artist at inducing people to reveal their inner selves. She sighed. "Poor, *poor* Ted."

"Sunny!" Freedkin said so emphatically she looked up. He sat next to her, dropped the open paper on her lap again and tapped Chance's picture with a long finger. "Sunny, I've got it."

"Got what?"

"The perfect solution to our ratings slump." He sprang up and began to pace. "I had a mud-wrestling bit in mind for next week's 'On the Town with Sunny' segment, but this is better—" He whooped and slapped his thigh. "Much better!"

Better than mud-wrestling? This was sounding bad. "Steve," Sunny glanced at her watch. "The show, remember? We go on in five minutes."

Steve dropped to his knees beside her and took both her hands. "Sunny Tyler's going to even the score!"

"What score?" she said suspiciously. "With whom?"

"With him." Freedkin released one hand long enough to jab at Chance again. "With *him*. He took a shot at you, now you take one at him. It's the American way."

"Steve, I don't think—"

"Yessss . . ." His eyes glazing manically, Steve patted her other hand. "Trust me, Sunny, *this will work*. Both shows have a live talk-show format. He goes on at nine, we go on at nine-thirty. By the end of the week even his hard-core viewers will be switching to us to see what you're going to say next. Oh my God," he groaned ecstatically. "Sheer genius."

"No," said Sunny, shaking her head as Steve began to pace and plan again.

"You're going to need a great line," he stressed, oblivious to her refusal, "something funny, a snappy comeback to Chance's Ken and Barbie crack."

"No!"

Freedkin froze. His head snapped around.

Sunny froze too. Had she just bellowed "no"? *Sunny Tyler? Famous for her smile and her disposition—a good sport who never complained, even when waitresses brought her tuna instead of egg salad?*

"You're kidding," Steve said, fully recovered now, beginning to grin.

Sunny stood up, the paper sliding to the floor. She'd never refused any of his schemes before, no matter how lunatic, but this she couldn't do. "No, Steve, I'm not kidding. I won't be a party to a petty public exhange of insults."

"A petty public exchange of insults," he echoed thoughtfully. His features began to glow; his eyes rolled. "I love it, I love it! Now all we have to do is think of something—"

"Steven, I warn you. I'll never lower myself to Graham Chance's level." She looked at her watch and started for the door.

He got there first and blocked her exit. "Lower yourself, I beg you," he rasped. "Sometimes we have to stoop to conquer."

At her recalcitrant expression, he began to whisper. "Sunny, I don't think you realize what's at stake here. Bill Blanchard is interested in our show."

"Bill Blanchard?" Sunny felt the color draining from her face. The vice-president of programming for RBC?

Steve clapped a hand over her mouth. "Shhhh—if it gets out now, we've blown the whole thing."

"Interested?" she mumbled through his fingers.

He nodded, left her leaning awestruck against the door, and began to pace again. "RBC's looking for an upbeat afternoon talk show; Blanchard's assistant called me last week—nothing definite yet, just talk."

"What kind of—" her voice dropped to a whisper at the producer's throat-cutting gesture "—talk?"

"Let's just say he's very interested." Steve's hand flew up dramatically. "But how long can it last with Chance stealing our thunder? His talk show is filching our ratings points on a daily basis. Let's face it, Graham Chance isn't just candid, he's outspoken, he's courageous, the public loves him. Dammit, Sunny, enough of this good sport stuff. It's time to take a stand. Defend your position; match him, best him!"

Sunny felt a lump the size of Texas lodge in her throat. A network talk show? A nationwide audience? In her wildest dreams she hadn't expected...

A sharp rap on the door made her start. "Sunny! Steve!" an assistant producer called. "Forty-five seconds."

"Right there," Steve yelled back. "Listen," he pressed, grabbing her by the arms, "at the show's closing you're gonna look straight into that camera and send Graham Chance a zinger. Dazzle him with a smile and then flatten him with a one-liner."

"I can't, Steve," she said hoarsely. "It's not me, it's not my style. I don't do one-liners."

"Don't worry about that. I'll come up with something. Just read the cue cards."

Something told her this could backfire—and backfire big. She had more than just herself to think about. There was Ted. His career. The U.S. Congress! "No, Steve, I can't do it." She implored the producer to understand, then realized how futile that was. Steve Freedkin was L.A. television's newest wunderkind. His meteoric career leaps had been accomplished by taking incredible risks and by a single-minded disdain for caution.

She took a deep breath and squared her shoulders. "I can't do it, Steve. There's Ted, there's...too much at stake." Pulling free of his grasp, she jerked the door open and rushed down the hall to the set.

Sunny welcomed the station break that preceded her last segment with a sigh of relief. She was nearly through. Just one more interview—Georgia Greene—a flamboyantly funny comedienne who never stopped talking, thank goodness. Once Georgia got started, Sunny's only requirement was to be a straight woman and laugh on cue. That she could handle.

The bustle around her claimed Sunny's attention. The floor manager began the countdown to airtime. The mobile microphone boom swung around to settle several feet above the modular couch Sunny was perched on. Off set to her left, Steve Freedkin talked with Georgia, while the comedienne waited to be introduced.

"... three, two, one..." The red light blinked on, and Sunny flashed the camera a sparkling smile. "And now I've got a real treat for you," she said breathlessly. "My next guest is one of the funniest women in America." As Sunny stood up the comedienne swept in, laughing, blowing kisses to the camera and crew.

"You're looking wonderful, Georgia," Sunny said, a little taken aback by the woman's extravagant style.

"I *am* wonderful, darling, ask my chauffeur," the comedienne gurgled, letting her laughter escalate into the high-pitched trilling that was her trademark. "Or my last husband, if they've released him from the home." Another peal of laughter tapered off as Georgia leaned back, draped her arm along the back of the sofa and leveled a stare at Sunny. "But enough about me, darling, it's you who's got the town all abuzz. Sunny Tyler feuding? I'm speechless."

If only that were true, Sunny lamented silently, then reminded herself that the feud business was bound to come up sooner or later. Might as well get it over with now—let Georgia and the viewers see she didn't intend to give such significance a moment's airtime. Rallying with what she hoped was disarming laughter, she wagged a finger at her guest. "Oh no you don't, Georgia. I ask the questions, remember? Besides, there *is* no feud." She shook her head. "None, nothing, *nada*."

"Oh, really?" Georgia looked like a chicken hawk sighting its dinner. "Well, I can tell you this: if Graham Chance had compared *me* to a windup toy, there'd be a feud."

Sunny felt irritation build. Always the professional, she fought it down. "It was a Barbie doll," she corrected, her voice prickling. "And Graham Chance is hardly responsible for what's happened. He merely made an observation about Ted and me. It's the media who's turned it into a national joke—'' Sunny stopped abruptly. Why was she defending Graham Chance?

The comedienne winked as though she'd read Sunny's mind. "Rushing to the man's defense? How interesting."

"I'm not rushing anywhere," Sunny insisted, flustered. Exactly how and when had she lost control of this situation?

"Just how well do you know him?" Georgia asked.

"Hardly at all—or rather—not at all, that is." Sunny felt color warm her cheeks. "I've seen his show...once or twice." Her face grew hotter and irritation began to percolate like brewing coffee. This was all *his* fault. Store clerks, grocery checkers and virtual strangers weren't enough. Now her very own guests were harassing her about Graham Chance's snide remarks! Sunny's palms became damp. Color mottled her face and neck. And a week's worth of suppressed anger emerged like steam escaping from a kettle.

"My, what healthy color," Georgia observed puckishly, then at Sunny's mute irritation, coaxed, "You know what they say about silence, dear. It's damning."

Sunny tossed her hair defiantly and cleared her throat. "I told you, I don't know Graham Chance at all—" She should have stopped right there, *but she couldn't.* "And with any luck, I never will," she muttered. Her eyes flashed to the camera. "But if you should happen to be listening, Mr. Chance, a word of advice: clean up your act. A first-rate interview would do more for your ratings than taking cheap shots at your competition." As spontaneously as she'd begun, Sunny halted, horrified by the rapidly approaching camera. *What was she doing?*

Survival instincts took over. A wan smile surfaced. She swallowed hard. "And now," she said, her voice cracking slightly, "please stay tuned. We'll be right back with more of *L.A. Heartbeat.*"

Pandemonium broke loose on the set. An assistant producer rushed up as Sunny sagged against the couch. Georgia, fanning herself with her hat, apologized profusely. "I'm fine," Sunny insisted weakly in response to the production staff's nervous buzzing. "Everything's fine."

Daphne, the makeup artist, hovered, ready to blot away any overt signs of trauma with Pan Cake.

"Sunny," boomed a voice from the booth. She looked up to see Steve Freedkin giving her a thumbs-up sign.

"...three, two, one..." the floor manager counted. *I've been had,* Sunny realized, smiling dazedly as the red light flashed on.

The next morning at exactly 9:00 A.M., Sunny locked her dressing room door, turned on the small, portable television set and switched to a rival channel. She didn't want Steve Freedkin or any of the crew to know just how anxious she was to hear Graham Chance's reaction, if any, to her *advice.* As the show's soft-rock theme and opening promos started, Sunny's insides went light again with that disturbing weightless sensation. A moment later an upper-torso shot of the source of her nervous stomach filled the screen.

"Good morning," he said, his blue eyes directed right at Sunny. "I'm Graham Chance, welcome to *Take a Chance.* We've got an unusual show for you today—" As he went on to name the guests scheduled for his own particular brand of in-depth interview, Sunny took a deep breath, flicked the TV off and began to pace. He wasn't going to say anything, and even if he did, she didn't want to hear it. Damn him anyway for starting this whole silly business, and double damn Steve Freedkin for tricking her into—no, that wasn't fair, Steve hadn't tricked her. Or at least he said he hadn't. He'd sworn on his sainted mother's life that he had nothing to do with Georgia asking those questions.

Sunny sighed. It was her own temper that had provoked her, and she was as shocked at the outburst as everyone else. Sunny Tyler snapping at a television camera? Unthinkable. Her image was upbeat and effervescent.

Without thinking, she paced past the set and flicked it on again. Chance's confident smile reappeared. Why did he have to seem so self-possessed, so quietly in command? His training in psychology seemed to have armed him with a cool, analytical ability to read people that unnerved her.

She squinted at the screen. His features could never be considered attractive taken separately—his face was too long, his chin too blunt, his nose a bit crooked—but taken together, they were devastating. The Kennedyesque waves of golden-brown hair, the sun bleached eyebrows and ardently blue eyes. Feud or no feud, that face seemed designed to set feminine hearts adrift.

He's a brazen opportunist, she reminded herself. He makes headlines off innocent people's weaknesses and flaws, always probing for personal secrets, for disclosures that are none of his business. Look what he's done to me, to Ted!

Her chin set grimly as her eyes refocused on the popular television figure. "Before we bring on our first guest," Chance said, a wry amusement playing about his mouth, "I feel compelled to comment on Sunny Tyler's advice. For those of you who haven't heard, Miss Tyler, host of *L.A. Heartbeat* on another local channel, chided me yesterday for taking cheap shots at my competition, presumably meaning herself." His mouth eased in a charmingly ironic grin; his blue eyes almost crackled. "I didn't know God gave Miss Tyler a temper like the rest of us. Was it just a fluke, or is there some real spunk under those 'bubbles'?"

Bubbles? Sunny felt a nerve near her eye twitch.

Sobering a little, Chance leaned back. "Even though I may couch my interview questions in humor, I seek the truth and I tell the truth, *always*, and if Miss Tyler considers that a cheap shot—'' he raised a hand ''—I have no defense.''

His eyes began to sparkle again as he looked straight in the camera. ''Just for the record, Sunny—if you're watching—I'm impressed. I've always been a sucker for scrappy charm, even when I'm the target. And not to worry, a little honest anger won't short out that beautiful smile.''

With an appreciative nod, he turned to the business of introducing his first guest.

Her face warm, her breathing shallow, Sunny stared at the TV screen, paralyzed by a fit of ambivalence. What had he just done? Bubbles, scrappy charm, honest anger, beautiful smile? Were those supposed to be compliments? Had she been praised or patronized?

Oh, God. Why was her heart doing sambas, rhumbas, all manner of Latin syncopations? She flicked off the TV and sank down on the couch with an exhaled moan. How could she ever respond to him now? Was she angry . . . or a teensy bit pleased? In truth, she was both, and much more. Embarrassed, off balance, perfectly furious, *intrigued*. Simple, uncomplicated Sunny Tyler was a mess of conflicting emotions.

By four o'clock Sunny's mixed feelings had resolved themselves into one resounding theme: she was angry. Her dressing room phone had rung incessantly, with everyone from her immediate family to avaricious members of the press clamoring to know her reaction to Chance's remarks. Freedkin, the show's director and various members of the production staff had hounded her shamelessly trying to find out what she intended to do. Rumor had it that even KRBC's station manager had been contacted by the press for a policy statement on the Tyler-Chance feud. Did KRBC condone such goings-on? . . . they wanted to know.

Oh yes, Sunny was angry. She couldn't remember ever being so angry before. And what was she going to do about it? The nervous twitch moved her lower lids. *Exactly nothing.*

"That's right," she told Steve Freedkin, as she paused at the door, jacket and purse in hand. "I'm not going to answer Graham Chance. And I'm not going to say another word about this whole fiasco, on or off the air. That man has turned my life into a zoo, Steve, and I'll never forgive him for that, but I am not going to fight with him for the prurient benefit of the press or the public. No—" she shook her head as Freedkin's myopic brown eyes implored her "—not for ratings, not for a network show, not for any other reason."

With another head shake, she hurried down the hall, stunned at her own assertiveness, and only too aware that if Steve followed her, if he pressured her, she'd fall like a house of cards. The only thing that kept her strong was an ominous premonition that if she gave in, if she let herself engage in an airwaves skirmish with Chance, the situation could quickly escalate beyond her control. She didn't know why, or how, she just knew she couldn't let it happen.

As she rushed from the studio and into the parking lot, she found herself dead center in the approach path of a disturbingly familiar figure. The moment it took her eyes to refocus decided her fate. It was too late. Graham Chance had seen her.

He stopped a moment, as though considering, and in that brief pause she had the impulse to run, to run like crazy.

"Sunny Tyler?" he asked, as though not quite sure. His smile was disarmingly friendly, his eyes curious and *very* blue.

Should she deny it? Did she dare shake her head and walk right past him?

But he was already moving toward her, and his expression had lost its uncertainty. She tried not to notice the style—call it casual flair—with which he moved. And the incredible fit of his clothes. Was it possible to be preppy and

outdoorsy and distinguished all at once? His navy cash-
mere sweater, pale blue shirt and off-white slacks answered
"yes." His sunstreaked hair and golden tan made it unani-
mous. *Wow* was the first word that came to mind. *Hunk* was
the next.

"It is Sunny Tyler, isn't it?" he asked, stopping within
touching distance of her.

Talking was out of the question. She told her head to nod
and was infinitely grateful when it complied.

He held out a hand as though they were about to be great
friends. "I'm Graham Chance."

"I...know." She took his hand. It was warm and strong.
That twitch in her eye had started again.

Their clasped hands lingered a moment. Another half-
beat passed before she could break from the pull of his
gaze...and still another slipped by before she could collect
herself enough to think of something to say. And then she
said it so...bluntly. "Why are you here?"

His eyes sparkled a little, but mostly they were soft and
blue as cornflowers. "Curiosity," he said amiably, "and
business."

"Curiosity?"

"I suppose I've always wanted to see what KRBC looked
like from the inside. You know, rival station and all that."

"And the business?" *Such eloquence.* She grimaced
mentally. *He'll think English is my second language.*

A smile touched his lips. "Is this an interview? Maybe I
should have a mike on."

A telling warmth seeped up her neck. "Sorry," she said
covering. "It's habit. I'd interview the delivery boy if he'd
let me."

His eyes brushed over her. "He's a fool if he doesn't."

Her color deepened, and Chance's eyes flicked away as
though he was a little embarrassed himself. "By the way,"
he said, after a moment, "in case you didn't catch my show
this morning—"

"I caught it."

"Oh?" He laughed. "To what do I owe the honor? You're not a closet fan?" His eyes were vibrant and energy-giving.

Suddenly, inexplicably, she felt quite brave. "You know very well why I watched."

Their eyes connected with a brief spark of meaning, an unspoken exchange that sent her heart on a crazy journey.

His smile deepened and he studied her intently. "I meant what I said this morning. There's a lot of fire and flash under that smile. You ought to allow yourself that kind of spontaneity more often."

She felt her stomach tighten again. What did he mean by that? Was he patronizing her? "I consider myself *very* spontaneous."

His gaze flickered now, piercing.

Tensing, Sunny realized she was dealing with a man who could strip back emotional defenses with a look. Her breathing faltered.

"It may be more television's fault than your own, Sunny," he acknowledged bluntly, "but that smile is one of the few spontaneous things about you. That and the anger you expressed yesterday."

Astonishment splotched her face with color. "I prefer to keep my fire and flash to myself, thank you," she defended. "There's no place for uncontrolled outbursts on television." Her eye twitched maddeningly. "And I wasn't angry," she insisted stiffly. "I was merely offering some sorely needed advice."

"Just like you're not angry now?"

It was a moment before she could speak. "Yes," she croaked indignantly, "just like now."

Her body tensed as his eyes assessed her, slowly, deliberately. "Constricted pupils, flushed skin, a slight facial tic? Those are all signs of arousal, Sunny. Sympathetic nervous system arousal, to put it technically. You're either angry or—"

"I'm not angry," she insisted, "and I'm certainly not *or.*"

He laughed softly and the blue of his eyes deepened. Penetrating hers, they seemed to read every secret she'd ever had. She felt as though her emotions were being systematically monitored, gauged and measured.

His hand lifted and Sunny had a sharp premonition that he meant to touch her, to slide a hand around her waist, to draw her close...

She waited, frozen.

He flicked his wrist over and glanced at his watch. "I have to go," he said quietly.

She nodded, feeling like a perfect fool as he smiled, turned and walked toward the building. Staring after him, she felt the telltale quiver near her eye with her fingertips and covered it, pressing hard. And to think that for one impulsive minute she'd actually thought she might learn to *like that man.*

Two

"A menu, ma'am?" the red-jacketed waiter asked.

"Not yet, thanks." Brushing at her angora sweater dress, Sunny flashed him a nervous smile. "I'm meeting someone."

With a nod he moved away and Sunny resumed her watch on the restaurant's entrance. She'd picked this West Los Angeles cubbyhole because of its tantalizing canneloni and its relative obscurity. The last thing she wanted was to be spotted by anyone, especially the press. It was Ted's first trip back to California from Washington, and he was upset enough about all the hoopla.

Crossing her legs, Sunny felt little snaps of electricity in the peach-colored dress as she smoothed the skirt back down over her knees. She wanted to be perfect tonight. Ted seemed so aware of her appearance since he'd found the political spotlight.

At least she could assure him that she'd tried to put an end to the feud business. She'd neither watched Graham

Chance's show nor uttered the man's name since running into him that afternoon at KRBC two weeks ago. On the contrary, despite crushing pressure, Sunny'd stuck to her vow of silence regarding Chance. She'd even ignored the speculation about his visit and the rumors that the KRBC brass had asked Chance to back off—to take the pressure off Sunny, their potential network star. If only that were true!

Unfortunately, Chance's occasional wry comments and Sunny's stubborn silence seemed to fuel the media's curiosity. They hounded her, waiting for her outside KRBC's gated entrance with camera crews and flashbulbs. And now Sunny was sure this impromptu trip of Ted's to L.A. had something to do with her notoriety.

Her heart jumped nervously as the restaurant door swung open. Instinctively she smiled and stood up, then felt an odd breeze and looked down. Had her dress come up with her? Folds of angora seemed to have attached themselves to her lap. The hitched-up skirt clung to her slip, which in turn clung to her nylons, the whole mess crackling audibly as she tried to ease it down. What a time for a case of static cling!

A young couple came through the door and Sunny sank back down, did a double take and stood up again as Ted entered right behind them. "Over here," she called, smiling and trying to unobtrusively separate her dress from her slip.

Despite the awkward situation, a familiar pleasure warmed her at the sight of her fiancé's solid stature and conservative good looks. Brown hair, gray eyes, square chin . . . Ted never changed.

Sunny didn't want to call out again and attract attention, but Ted didn't seem to see her. She slipped out of the booth and started toward him, her dress hugging her legs, crawling upward. When she tried to tug it down, the angora stuck to her hand. She froze. The dress was alive. One more step and she'd be doing a commercial for panty hose! Aware of the curious stares of the other patrons, she began to edge back toward the booth.

Finally Ted saw her. He reached her in seconds, took off his blue suit jacket, wrapped it around her and hurried her back to their table. "What have you got on?" he questioned as they sat down.

Every movement prickled as she maneuvered into the booth and fought to get the dress back down to her knees.

"Sunny, really," he murmured irritably, slipping his jacket back on. "Short styles may be popular again, but do you think it's in your best interests—*or mine*, for that matter, to wear them?" His brows flattened as he brushed peach-colored angora from his lapel.

Before she could explain, the waiter appeared with menus, his eyes widening in surprise. "Hey, aren't you—?" he started.

"See," Ted muttered, nudging Sunny, "all that carrying-on has got you recognized. Now we won't have a moment's peace."

"No *you*," the waiter insisted, waving the menus at Ted. "Aren't you that ex-NFL quarterback, uh, Ed somebody?"

"Ted Walsh," Ted corrected.

"Yeah!" The waiter slapped the menus against his leg. "Hey, this is great. Can I have an autograph?"

Resisting a wicked urge to nudge Ted back, Sunny watched him grab the waiter by the hem of his jacket and pull him close. Her mouth dropped open. What had gotten into her steady, placid fiancé?

"Keep it down," Ted warned, releasing the young man long enough to pull a scrap of paper from his suit pocket, scribble an autograph and offer it to the waiter along with a ten-dollar bill. "We don't want to be disturbed, okay?"

"Hey, sure," the waiter said, nodding. "It's cool. These lips are sealed. Nobody's ever gonna know that Ted Walsh was in the place with—" He squinted at Sunny curiously.

"Goldie Hawn," she whispered.

His eyes bulged, and Ted grabbed him by the jacket again. "She's only kidding," he hissed, pressing another ten in the waiter's hand. "Now get us two orders of canneloni and a liter of Chianti *fast*—and not one word!"

The waiter backed away with a dazed nod. "Sure, a liter of canneloni, right away."

He disappeared around the corner and Ted slanted a dark look at Sunny.

"Sorry," she said automatically, then let out the breath she'd been holding and retorted, "You didn't have to tell him your name."

"The guy recognized me," Ted insisted lamely, picking strands of angora off his sleeve. His sour expression put an end to the discussion.

If their evening was to be successful at all, Sunny knew she'd have to smooth things over quickly. Ted must have been under terrible pressure. His sense of humor seemed to have vanished since his interview with Graham Chance, and although he'd never said it in so many words, she suspected he'd begun to blame the entire mess on her.

"It's been a month since we've seen each other, Ted," she said quietly, offering her hand. "Let's not fight."

After a moment he sighed and took her hand.

"I'm glad you're back." She smiled as he leaned over and kissed her lightly.

"Sunny, we have to talk."

"I know," she agreed, "but can't it wait until we've had dinner and a moment to get reacquainted?"

The waiter returned with their wine and food, served it and hovered as though he couldn't tear himself away. Ted pulled out another ten. "Keep up the good work," he said, smiling bleakly as he stuck the money in the young man's pocket and signaled him away with a nod of his head. "Eat fast," he muttered to Sunny, "or I'll be broke before we get the bill."

Sunny muffled a chuckle and quickly held up her wine-glass for a toast. "To us," she said, clinking her glass against his.

The meal progressed uneventfully despite an undercurrent of strain. Ted discoursed on his trials and tribulations "on the hill" while Sunny listened attentively. Neither mentioned the feud.

As she finished the last delicious bite of her canneloni and pushed the plate away, the waiter hurried over to take it. "Thanks," she said smiling, vaguely aware of a change in the restaurant's atmosphere. Nudging Ted, she glanced around. The other guests were openly quite staring, and unoccupied waiters and busboys hovered in spectator clumps.

Through his politician's smile Ted hissed at the waiter, "I thought you weren't going to tell anyone."

"I didn't," he insisted, then looked around and shrugged. "Okay, I called my girlfriend and maybe somebody overheard me. But she would have killed me if—"

"She'll have to wait her turn," Ted muttered. "I'm going to kill you first."

"Relax," the waiter soothed. "I'll get you out of here. Forget the bill, you've already given me eno—"

Sunny gasped as the door swung open behind him, and two reporters from one of the gossip rags sauntered in. She nudged Ted hard, so hard he expelled a startled gust of air. "Over there," she said, pointing frantically. The entire restaurant turned as one to stare at the newcomers.

Their waiter glanced over his shoulder. "Don't worry," he whispered, obviously beginning to enjoy his part in the drama. "I'll take care of them. You guys can get out that way." He pointed to a hallway behind them.

"Does it lead to the back door?" Sunny questioned.

"No, the rest rooms. There's a window above the trash can—"

"Never mind," said Ted. "We'll take our chances with the reporters."

"No," Sunny warned. She knew those two men; they were jackals. They wouldn't let up until they'd provoked Ted to a fist fight or worse. "Stall them," she ordered the waiter, grabbing a handful of Ted's suit jacket. *"Come on."*

Crouching, they dashed down the hall. As they burst into the ladies' room, a woman screamed and flattened herself against the wall. "What is it? A fire?" she croaked.

Sunny shook her head helplessly. "No, no," she soothed with the only excuse that came to mind. "Italian food always affects him this way."

"Sunny," Ted warned. He pushed the trash can aside and positioned himself under the partially open window to give her a leg up.

Witnessing Ted's serious face and crouching posture made something in Sunny want desperately to laugh. But she couldn't let them get caught this way! Heedless of her bunched dress, she darted over and let herself be boosted up to the windowsill. With a little pressure, the pane easily pushed open. Swinging her legs up and over, Sunny stared down and froze. It was so dark she couldn't see the ground. How much of a drop was it?

"Hey, you're in my way!" Ted warned, grunting as he hoisted his stocky body up and forced her off the ledge.

"Oh, no!" she cried, dropping, hitting the ground with a soft thud and tumbling to her knees. The earth shook as Ted landed a fraction of an inch to her right. Any closer, she realized, shuddering, and she'd be in the record books, a grim statistic.

"I took a taxi," he hissed.

"My car's on Hamilton," she whispered back.

Moments later, they crept into her Karman Ghia and headed toward the freeway, Sunny driving.

She jumped when Ted leaned over and put a hand on her shoulder. "This has got to stop," he warned tightly.

"What, Ted?" she asked, confused, concentrating on the rearview mirror.

"This whole crazy business. You've got to stop fighting on television, climbing out of windows, wearing short dresses, oh God—" he groaned "—showing up in the gossip tabloids every day. I don't think you realize how it affects *me*, Sunny. I'm losing credibility!"

"Ted, I'm sorry." She truly was. Guilt knotted her stomach. She'd never seen him like this. He must be under a terrible strain.

"I want you to quit your job and marry me, Sunny, *now*. This weekend."

She hit the brakes just in time to avoid running a red light. Her hands frozen on the wheel, she breathed, "Ted, never make jokes like that when a person's driving."

"I'm serious. A politician needs a wife, a helpmate, a supporter—"

"Ted, darling," she soothed anxiously. "We agreed that we'd marry some time next year, that I'd continue working for a while to give my career a fair chance." How could she tell him she was being considered for a network show, that she couldn't possibly quit now!

"I've reconsidered. I think we should marry now. Okay," he conceded, "maybe this weekend is a bit precipitous—but soon. We'll put a stop to all this mindless media sensationalism."

His grip on her shoulder was becoming oppressive. Ted wasn't the only one under pressure. She'd been under plenty of stress, endured harrassment from every direction and now from him, too? Everybody wanted Sunny to do what *they* wanted Sunny to do—even Ted. A bitter lump formed in her throat. Her romantic nature would never mesh with a quickie marriage as a means to an end. "Are you staying at the Hyatt?" she asked, veering onto the freeway off-ramp before he'd had a chance to answer.

"Yes . . . but I thought we'd go to your place."

"Not a good idea," she said curtly. "The rag reporters will probably be there."

"Ummm." He nodded in agreement. "Good thinking. The last thing I need now is a color picture in every super-market from here to Poughkeepsie." He chuckled as though it was a good joke.

She pulled the Karman Ghia up to the Hyatt's entrance.

"You're coming in aren't you?" He stroked her knee suggestively.

"Not a good idea," she repeated, feeling a startling urge to slap his hand away. "Someone might see us."

Unknowingly, he lifted his hand just in time to avoid in-jury. "Sunny, I'm serious about moving up the wedding. You do agree don't you?"

"I don't know, Ted," she said putting him off. "It's been a rough night. I'm tired."

"Sure," he said sympathetically. "You go on home. Get a good night's rest. You'll see I'm right."

As she drove away, her stomach knotted with a confused bundle of emotions, and one that was becoming all too fa-miliar—anger. She was angry at Ted for his self-serving proposal and at herself for not having the gumption to tell him how she felt. She had no intention of quitting her job or getting married soon. The knot in her stomach pulled even tighter as she felt a disturbing glimmer of awareness. For the first time in their long and steady sojourn through high school and college, Sunny experienced an unthinkable thought. Was it possible that she might not want to marry Ted Walsh at all?

By Sunday afternoon, Sunny'd mustered the courage to tell Ted *most* of the truth—that she would not quit her job or move up the marriage, and that she needed time to think. By Sunday evening, Ted had packed and flown back to Washington, D.C., in a purple huff.

Sunny slipped on her new dandelion-yellow suit and matching pumps, then turned to her wardrobe mirrors and fluffed out her hair. In the past month she'd changed somehow, she realized, studying herself. She even looked different. Ever since taking a stand with Ted, she'd begun to feel some semblance of order in her life again. The press had calmed down; Ted was over his tiff and even their engagement was back on.

She looked down at the letter from her parents, lying open on her dresser top. After all the usual news about family, friends and the wet weather in San Francisco, her mother'd come right to the point. "Your father and I are so relieved that all the dreadful things we've been reading in the papers aren't true. You know we love Ted, dear, and how much we're looking forward to a wedding. Soon, we hope?" The letter ended with a P.S. that delicately questioned Sunny's shaggy hairdo.

Sunny sighed, pursed her lips and refolded the letter. Her parents were the doting kind, and if they overdid it at times, their intentions were good.

She took another look in the mirror and shook her head. Golden wisps floated and settled into a disordered mane. "I like it," she murmured. A shiver of excitement stirred her. She felt good about today. Life had begun to feel terrific again. Especially since this was the day she was scheduled to meet her new co-host!

Hurrying out of her Santa Monica condo, Sunny let herself into the Karman Ghia and started the engine. Sometimes Steve Freedkin's schemes were sheer genius, she decided buoyantly, negotiating the heavy commuter traffic. And this was one of those times.

Aware that Bill Blanchard wanted a fast-paced talk-and-variety show with male and female co-hosts, Steve had decided to revamp, *L.A. Heartbeat* into an exact replica of Blanchard's vision. They'd been interviewing and testing potential partners for Sunny for the past three weeks and had narrowed it down to four of the original fifty applicants.

Sunny's strong favorite, Ryan Forbes, a singer and television personality, was a shoo-in according to the rumors. And Steve, despite his adamant refusal to publicly reveal the name, had privately confided to Sunny that Forbes would be the pick.

She took a deep breath as she pulled up to the guard house at the KRBC entrance, waved at the attendant and drove through. Today the mystery would be over. She and the show's audience would meet her new co-host on live television. She couldn't remember being this nervous before!

Steve was already pacing the floor of her dressing room when she walked in. "Relax," she reassured him with a calmness she didn't feel. "Everything will go fine. Ryan and I tested out beautifully."

"Sunny, I—" He grabbed hold of her arm. "Come on, I want you to meet . . . him."

"Now?" she balked. "Why not do it on the air like we planned?"

Shaking his head, Steve pulled her down the hall to a spare office that now sported a gold star on the door. "Sunny," he whispered, hesitating, his hand on the knob. "We've been through a lot together, right? You and me? The lean years, fighting for every ratings point, doing whatever we had to do to make this show a success, to build careers. Not just yours and mine, but everybody's, the staff, the production crew—they all depend on us, on *you*, Sunny."

That hollow feeling assailed her stomach. "Steven," she whispered, "what's going on?"

"Sunny, promise you'll love me no matter what?"

Her palms began to sweat. "What have you done?"

He tapped on the door lightly and swung it open. Daphne was bending over the occupied makeup chair muttering to herself as she worked.

Steve cleared his throat. As Daphne swung around, exposing the occupant of the chair, Sunny began to back away. "No," she breathed. "Steven, *nooo*."

Her new co-host sat up, brushed his golden-brown hair back from his forehead and met her astonished gaze with a flickering smile.

"This can't be," she whispered, her voice cracking. "You already have a show. You're on another channel."

Graham Chance shrugged and the smile touched his famous blue eyes. "You haven't been reading the papers. My contract with KNBS ran out last week. My manager advised me not to renew. He felt this show had more potential—"

Sunny's throat locked with a cry of denial. Still backing away, her protest tumbled out in incoherent squeaks. She whirled on Steve, mute with horror. "W-was this your idea?" she blurted finally. "How long have you known, planned it?"

"Not long," he said, hunching his shoulders.

"How could you?"

"Sunny," Chance broke in firmly, reassuringly, "it's a job, nothing more, an hour a day."

She swallowed a moan. Graham Chance was to be the voice of reason in this fiasco? That was more insult than she could stand to have added to her injury. My God, she thought, turning away, she'd been betrayed, duped, used. She felt like a trapped animal. Had everyone known but her? *What should she do now?*

Brushing off Steve's hand, she hurried to her dressing room. Right behind her, Steve pushed the door open despite the weight of her entire body pressing against it. "Okay, I'm an idiot. I should have told you. Scream at me, hit me, bruise me, but promise me you won't do anything drastic."

"How could you, Steve?" she whispered, verging on angry tears.

He loped to the coffee table, picked up the day's script and waved it in a dramatic arc. "With Chance as your co-host, this show is a rocket to the stars. We're contenders for the big time, Sunny, center ring—" Dropping the script, he took her arms and shook her gently. "Don't you know what that means for you, for all of us? *I had to do it*. I had to get you the hottest co-host in town! Sunny," he whispered, shaking her again. "You and Chance are hot copy. By tonight you'll be in every entertainment column in the nation."

"Oh, God . . . *Ted*," she groaned.

He dropped her arms. "What's Ted got to do with this? Let him get his own media blitz."

A bracing male voice came from the open doorway. "I think she's trying to tell you she's concerned about Ted's political future, his image."

Sunny's head snapped up. "And why shouldn't I be concerned about his image after you got through with it?"

Chance entered and put a hand on Steve's shoulder. "Let me talk to her," he offered quietly.

Steve nodded, checking his watch. "Thirty minutes to airtime," he advised nervously.

"I'll handle it," Chance said under his breath, easing Steve toward the door.

Sunny bristled. He'd *handle* it?

"Make nice, you two," Steve whispered and disappeared.

Sunny turned away, her chin lifting mutinously. If she didn't have a contract to honor she'd be out of here so fast—

"If you walk," Chance said, anticipating her, "you'll be jeopardizing a lot of jobs, letting a lot of people down."

"Knock off the guilt trip," she muttered. "Steve beat you to it." She heard him closing in from behind her and stiffened.

"Maybe you've been taking all the hype too seriously, Sunny," he suggested, his voice drifting low and sonorously past her ear. "We engaged in a little public sparring but never maliciously. And let's face it, the publicity has boosted both our careers." The fragrance of an expensive male cologne reached her nostrils as he moved closer. Was it Copenhagen, her favorite? "Why not give this a chance?"

"I—" She shook her head. "No."

"You're afraid of me," he stated quietly. "Why?"

The question left her speechless. She couldn't turn, couldn't answer. Silence stretched out to a brittle snapping point. "Afraid?" she rasped. "Don't be ridiculous. I don't like the way you operate, that's all. You and Steve, collaborating, conspiring, sneaking around behind my back." Her indignation rose with every word. "It has nothing to do with fear," she insisted, turning to face him. "I'm a professional, and I deserve professional treatment. Springing something like this on me is contemptible."

"Uh-uh," he said, shaking his head, moving even closer. "You knew all along that the co-host's identity was being kept a secret. It's too late to complain about unprofessionalism."

"Steve told me it was going to be Ryan Forbes," she admitted tersely.

"I see." He folded his arms. "Then you've got a right to be angry at him. At Steve," he clarified, "not me."

"I am angry at Steve," she grated, "angry enough to poison his oatmeal."

"Umm...more of that scrappy charm?" He nodded thoughtfully. "I like it."

A moan of pure frustration built within her. Maybe he'd like her scrappy homicidal tendencies when she went for his neck? No one, not even Steve, made her as crazy as this man did; how could she possibly work with him? "We can't be co-hosts," she blurted. "It'll never work."

"Why not?"

"You know as well as I do that you're on record as having ridiculed Ted and me—"

"That wasn't ridicule," he cut in. "It was an observation. You, yourself, corrected Georgia Greene on that point. No." He shook his head thoughtfully, scanning her face as though he were noticing something for the first time. "No, that's not what's bothering you, at least not entirely."

Her breath caught as his blue eyes intensified their scrutiny. He moved closer and took her arm. "You're afraid I'll see something you don't want seen, discover something you've neatly tucked away."

A ripple of apprehension left her wobbly. She didn't want to ask, but couldn't stop herself. "Like what?"

His intimate inspection of her blinking eyes, her mouth, her quickened breathing, brought an uncontrollable flush to her face; the warmth raced lower, spreading over her chest, rousing her breasts. His hand on her arm was their only physical connection, yet she felt threatened by him, *invaded by him*.

"A whole reservoir of feelings you haven't consciously acknowledged yet," he said, his voice oddly husky. "Emotions you don't want tapped. You're terrified, Sunny, not of me, but of losing control."

A staccato rap on the door catapulted her heart into her throat. She pulled free of his hold as Steve's anxious voice inquired, "Everything okay, guys? Sunny? It's time."

A fine-tuned trembling moved through her limbs. When she didn't answer, the door creaked open.

As her producer's worried face appeared, Sunny clasped her hands together and pressed, summoning steadiness. The tremor eased and a numbing calm began to take hold. "Yes, I know, Steve," she said, her voice barely audible. "It's time."

Without looking back at Chance, she made her way down the hall to the set, Steve bounding beside her. "Hey, I knew you'd come through," he said gratefully. "You're a pro. Now remember," he coached, "right after the teasers, you say, 'And now, the moment you've all been waiting for is here. Stay tuned, because right after this break, I'll introduce my new co-host.' Then you flash one of your fabulous smiles and we go to commercials. Got it?"

She nodded automatically, a coil of insecurity tightening in the pit of her stomach. *Was* she terrified of losing control?

She took her place on the set's couch, the last-minute bustle before airtime a distant drone in her ears.

The countdown seemed to take forever. Waiting, hands still clasped, she saw the red light blink on and knew her nightmare had come true. She couldn't . . . quite . . . smile.

"This is Sunny Tyler," she said woodenly, reading the cue cards word for word, "and boy have we got excitement for you today. We're starting our new information-and-entertainment format, and in a few moments, we'll be talking with a potential Olympic gymnast, a rock singer turned movie star, a sizzling new star of the nighttime soaps and a well-known health food advocate." Sunny hesitated. The next cue card held the lines Steve had coached her on—the teaser about her new co-host.

A crazy defiance took hold and before she quite knew what she was doing, she skipped the entire card and ad-libbed instead, "We're excited here at *L.A. Heartbeat* about our brand-new format, and we know you're going to love today's show." The corners of her mouth turned up a fraction as she hesitated, blinking, a delayed realization of what she'd just done sinking in. "So stay tuned," she said, her smile brightening. "And we'll be right back."

Even the frantic waves of the floor manager, the dancing cue-card girl and the omnipresent red light couldn't loosen Sunny's stubborn tongue. She stared into the camera, unblinking. After fifteen silent seconds, the floor manager signaled the break.

"Sunny," Steve boomed from the booth. "Why the hell didn't you read the cue-cards—?"

As Steve's diatribe continued, Sunny glanced to her left and saw Graham Chance waiting in the wings. His hands were driven into his pants pockets and he looked distinctly edgy, she decided. A giddy sensation pervaded her. Was he nervous? Did Sunny Tyler have Graham Chance sweating?

"Are you listening, Sunny?" Steve's voice cracked in frustration. "Forget the teaser. Introduce Chance as soon as we go on. Understand? Sunny...? Look at me!"

She squinted up at the gesticulating figure in the smoke-glass control booth.

"Two hundred thousand people are tuned in and waiting—" Steve shouted over the start of the countdown.

Savoring a dangerous feeling of power, Sunny glanced to her left again. Graham Chance's piercing stare was fixed on her, his features suffused with a tense immediacy.

"So introduce your new co-host, dammit!" Steve roared just before the red light flashed on.

Chance stiffened. His hand rifled through his hair.

Maybe I will and maybe I won't, Sunny mused, deliciously calm. She flashed the camera a brilliant smile. "Welcome back to *L.A. Heartbeat...*"

Three

———

Graham Chance's jaw clenched with tension as he returned Sunny's provocative glance. What in the hell was that woman doing? A low chuckle, almost a growl escaped his throat as he watched her blithely ignore the frantic "psssts" and signals of the floor manager and crew. She pressed on, introducing her first guest, a young collegiate gymnast who'd just won the national championships, and rose to greet him as though that was exactly what she was supposed to do.

Gray's eyes flicked up to the booth where Freedkin paced. He knew the producer had a massive investment in this new format. When he'd offered Gray the show, Freedkin had confided the network's interest, dangling that and a fat salary increase like carrots. He'd also confided that Blanchard, the programming chief, would be watching today. Gray's eyes flicked back to Sunny. *Watching this crazy woman kidnap the show and hold it for ransom.*

Uttering an expletive, Gray brushed gold-streaked waves back from his forehead. Sunny Tyler had both his own and Freedkin's television future in her hot little hand, and she was squeezing hard.

Maybe he'd come to the wrong conclusion about Miss Tyler. After his interview with Ted Walsh several weeks ago, he'd watched her show out of curiosity. He knew the kind of woman the Ted Walsh's of the world required. Nice enough guys, but with a strong need for the stereotypically feminine woman—a throwback to the fifties, the kind easily trained to be docile, to fetch and carry, to polish men's egos. Ted Walsh wanted a soft-spoken, soft-thinking arm adornment to enhance his political career. And at first glance, Gray admitted, Sunny Tyler seemed to fit the bill perfectly.

But the more he looked, the more he saw—something bubbling up from within her. An energy that was vibrant, and a little raw. A rebellious streak just beginning to show itself. When she gets in touch with those deep-seated feelings, she'll be a holy terror, he thought, an odd tightness constricting his stomach muscles...a match for any man.

As the cameras focused on the gymnast's reply to Sunny's question, she glanced Chance's way again, a brief flash of triumph in her eyes. A rush of blood warmed his veins. Fascination and a touch of awe diluted his anger. He was watching a woman experience her first taste of real power. On some level, she knows that she's taken control of the show—and she's not going to relinquish it easily, he realized. The lady's either slightly crazed or incredibly gutsy.

Gray looked at his watch. The segment would be over in a couple of minutes, and Freedkin was on his way down from the booth. Now it's going to hit the fan, he thought, clenching his jaw.

Freedkin strode to Gray's side, his thin features pinched with frustration. "Sorry about this, Chance," he grated, pushing his oversized glasses back on his nose. "I don't know what the hell's got into Sunny. She's always been such a good sport.''

Gray smothered a laugh. Good sport hardly defined the woman out there now. The hint of defiance in her eyes; the vibrancy in her features thoroughly intrigued him. She was untamed, unapproachable, an incredible challenge.

They waited tensely as Sunny thanked the gymnast, then announced the promos for the next segment without so much as a word about Chance. Freedkin muttered an expletive. "Don't worry," he reassured Gray. "I'll straighten this out.''

As the camera light blinked off, an aide rushed up to escort the gymnast off the set. The floor manager and two assistant producers surrounded Sunny, forcing Freedkin to push through. After a mumbled exchange, Freedkin blurted, "Either you introduce him, Sunny, or I'll come on camera and do it for you!''

Gray couldn't hear her reply, but it obviously didn't please Freedkin. He took her by the arm and hustled her off into a corner, talking frantically. A moment later, seconds before the show resumed, Sunny was back on the couch, poised and smiling, with Freedkin waiting, arms folded, off camera.

Gray stared up at the monitor as a head and shoulders shot of Sunny flicked on. She looked amazingly cool and professional; her smile was pleasant enough, but on closer inspection he detected a slight quiver near her right eye and something dangerous hidden in the soft hazel of her irises. Her disarrayed hair and slightly flushed features assailed him like an aphrodesiac. A twist of excitement brought his breath up short.

"Guess what, folks," she said conspiratorially, "my producer's been giving me frantic signals. It seems I forgot all about the new co-host." Her smile expanded. "I don't know how it slipped by me, but I promise not to keep you waiting a moment longer." She swung out an arm graciously as though welcoming a dignitary. "There simply aren't words to do this man justice, so I won't even attempt an introduction. Without further delay, let me bring out my new co-host, Graham Chance."

Gray hesitated. The woman had him off balance. Did he go out now or was she setting him up for something? Freedkin was signaling wildly for him to go on.

"Now I ask you," Sunny said, shrugging and smiling into the camera, "how does one forget a man like Graham Chance?"

"Quite easily, apparently," Gray muttered, stepping up onto the set to take her extended hand.

"It's a rare pleasure," she retorted with a cool nod of her head. "Do you prefer Graham, or—?"

"Gray," he said. Smiling, he turned to nod to the camera.

"You may call me Barbie," she murmured.

His head snapped back, but before he could respond, she'd let go of his hand and reseated herself on the couch. This should prove interesting, he decided warily. He joined her on the couch, ignoring an assistant producer's waves to move closer.

With only the faintest vestige of her famous smile apparent, Sunny addressed the camera. "I'm sure I was more surprised than any of you to learn that Graham Chance was to be my new co-host, and I'm very curious about the circumstances." She turned to Gray, pinpoints of mutiny in her eyes. "How does it feel to be working with the woman you've been carrying on a public feud with—according to the press?"

She gets points for a direct hit, Gray mused. He hesitated a second, then saw a way to deflect her. "Maybe it's time for a public truce?" he suggested, his eyes glinting. "Somebody once said that loving your enemies is a shrewd practice. It saves you from the wear and tear of evil passions...." Smiling obliquely, he let the words trail off.

"I see," she said, but obviously didn't see at all. It took her a moment to regroup. "Maybe you'd like to tell us how you landed the job, considering all your competition?" she inquired, a subtle challenge in her eyes.

Gray regarded her shrewdly. The studio clock ticked away. He wasn't about to be provoked into the exposé she was pushing for, no matter how long she let the questions hang. "I was hoping you had something to do with it," he replied evenly.

The assistant producer again signaled him to slide closer to Sunny, and this time he deliberately complied, feeling her stiffen as his knee brushed hers. His eyes traced the silky line of her thigh beneath the soft jersey skirt she wore, and a band of muscle tightened across his shoulders as he realized that another inch closer and the full length of that long sleek leg would be aligned against his.

"You must have some idea why you were chosen, Gray," she insisted politely. "Don't keep us in suspense."

Damn, he realized, she was using one of his own techniques on him. Interview chicken—repeat a tough question and remain silent until the interviewee was provoked into answering. "No, honestly, I don't," he lied. Adrenaline sharpened his senses at her continuing silence. Should he risk a standoff against this deranged rookie?

From off set to his left, Freedkin's threatening utterances zinged past Gray's ears. After several more seconds of dead air, Gray fought down his urge to conquer. Strangling this impudent woman bare-handed had tremendous appeal, but not with two hundred thousand witnesses to the assault. "Maybe we'd better bring on our next guest?" he suggested menacingly.

"Sounds like a great idea," she agreed, her voice breaking slightly. Her lower eyelid quivered noticeably now.

She's pushed past her limits, he realized with a twang of satisfaction. She's beginning to realize what she's done.

"Get ready for a thrill, music fans," she said, reading the cue cards. "We've got rock music's hottest idol, One-eyed Jack, and he's here to tell us about his new movie role . . ."

Gray watched her carefully, noting the slight tremor in her voice, the flushed skin revealed by the V neckline of her blouse. An errant thought struck him. What would it be like to undo that blouse one button at a time, to touch that silken fire? A tight sensation crowded the pit of his stomach.

Taking her cue, he stood as the silver-studded rock singer bounced onto the set. "Hello," Sunny said, extending her hand to the entertainer. The flash of her diamond engagement ring caught Gray's attention. A sudden awareness jarred him. *Sunny Tyler is someone else's woman.* He'd known all along, but the immediacy of the realization made it seem new and disturbing.

He shook the rock singer's hand absently.

One-eyed Jack seated himself next to Sunny and the camera angled in on them as she began the interview.

Watching her, listening to her, Gray felt an uncanny sensation, an echo from the past. His mind superimposed an image over Sunny's expressive features . . . the face of another woman. Memory rewound and played back in stark detail. A cord in his neck tightened. Kristin. She'd been engaged, too, but that hadn't stopped her from . . .

Their guest's laughter at something Sunny'd said broke through Gray's preoccupation. He smiled along with them, covering his distraction.

As his gaze focused on the woman next to him, on the strands of her pale gold hair glinting in the bright lights, on her fragrant scent, he felt the cords in his neck pull tighter. She aroused something powerful within him. . . .

An exaggerated movement brought her arm into contact with his and when she turned, startled, he caught a glimpse of something so vulnerable in her expression, his chest clutched like a fist.

"Are you a rock music fan, Gray?" she asked, her voice unsteady.

He nodded once, forcing a smile. "Raised on *American Bandstand.*"

As she turned away, he wrestled the dangerous responses under control. A muscle in his jaw contracted. She's not fair game, he reminded himself grimly, *and Graham Chance doesn't poach.*

With a tremorous exhale, Sunny sagged onto her dressing room couch. Her breathing came shallow, almost in pants, and her heart raced at what felt like sixty miles per hour. She must be mad to have tried such an insane thing. She was risking her career, her relationship with Ted . . . her very sanity. If she'd controlled herself, acted like a professional and brought the show off as planned, she'd have been infinitely better off. The media would have pounced on the story, and Ted would have fumed for a while, but eventually the dust would have settled.

But now? After what she'd just done? Hijacking the show, trashing her new co-host, provoking a verbal duel and playing off countless seconds of dead airtime? "Oh, Sunny," she groaned in despair, her hands framing her face. She had no defense except diminished capacity, and who was buying that one these days? She knew what she was supposed to do, but she couldn't do it, *she just couldn't.* Something inside her had gone a little crazy. Steve Freedkin's question reverberated in her mind: what's gotten into you, Sunny?

At the sound of approaching footsteps, she cringed and flattened out on the couch, facedown. She wasn't ready to face the inquisition yet, not in her present state of mind.

"Sunny?" Steve called, thumping vigorously on her door.

She pulled an armful of throw pillows over her head.

"Open up, dammit!" he boomed. The pounding continued, punctured by a kick or two. "Sunny, let me in!"

As the noise and explosive threats continued, she pushed the pillows aside. That didn't sound like the entire crew—armed to the teeth and led by Graham Chance—come to lynch her. Maybe it was just Steve?

The door creaked and groaned as a body thudded against it. "I'll break this door down if I have to!"

She sat up as another tremor hit the door, exhaled heavily and noted the wrinkled mess she'd made of her skirt. She even looked like a woman on the skids.

"Sunny!"

"It's open," she called absently.

The thudding stopped. "What?"

"The door's not locked."

The knob twisted tentatively before the door swung open. Standing on the threshold, Steve rubbed his arm. "Why the hell didn't you say so before I gave myself linebacker's shoulder?" Shaking his head, he walked in and stepped over the coffee table. "Sunny, have you gone crazy?"

Eyes downcast, she sighed. "I think so."

"Sunny, Sunny, Sunny," he moaned, dropping down on the couch beside her. "Do you have any idea what you've done?"

She nodded slowly.

"No, I don't think you do." He slapped his hand against his leg and sprang up. "Bill Blanchard was watching today. His aide just called and wanted to know whose taffy we thought we were pulling."

Sunny's heart sank like an anchor.

"Thank God the man has a sense of humor," Steve muttered. "I told him you were distraught, a death in the family."

"Umm." She nodded, beyond caring. After a moment, her eyebrows puckered, and she roused a little. "Why didn't you tell me Blanchard was watching?"

Steve scratched his forehead. "You mean I didn't?" He shrugged defensively. "Hell, I only had one thing on my mind—getting Sunny Tyler in front of the cameras. Thank God, Chance talked you out of jumping ship.''

"Steve," she blurted suddenly. "Do you have any idea why I did what I did?"

He lifted a hand, sincerely puzzled. "Female problems?"

She shook her head, annoyed.

His shoulders lifted. "I'm not good at guessing games. Nervous breakdown, maybe... your sex life? Ted's gay?" She shook her head again, and he pushed his glasses up on his nose to peer at her. "You're not trying to tell me it's burn-out? Come on, Sunny, that's today's fad excuse, everybody in the industry—"

"It's him."

"Who? Chance? He's burned out?"

"I'm serious," she warned. "He and I are the cat and dog of daytime television. We're natural enemies. We'll *never* be able to work together."

"Hey," he said reprovingly. "I don't like to hear words like 'never.' You and Gray are going to be great together. You just need a little time. There's chemistry working—"

"Chemistry leads to lab accidents," she prophesied grimly. With a pleading look in her eyes, Sunny walked over to him, took both his arms, just as he'd so often done to her, and shook him gently. "You're going to have to face the truth, Steve. You've chosen the wrong co-host. But don't worry, we can fix it. We'll replace Chance. Ryan Forbes is still available—"

His eyes narrowed as she continued to shake him. "You're in worse shape than I thought," he muttered. Shrugging off her hands, he grabbed and shook her back, none too gently this time. "This is it, Sunny. I'm through. No more Mr. Nice Guy. Compassion and sensitivity obviously aren't working, so I'm giving you twenty-four hours to get your act together, hear? I want you in this studio tomorrow morning and I want to see smiles, laughter, hilarity. I want to hear 'Good morning, Gray, it's a joy working with you.' I want joy, Sunny. I *demand* joy.''

He stopped shaking her and searched her face. "Can you do it?" He grabbed her chin and nodded her head in a vigorous 'yes.' "Sure you can, baby, you're a pro. Come on, Sunshine; give me one of your smiles," he coaxed, nodding, tickling her chin with his finger. "Come onnnnn—"

She couldn't resist him. A smile quirked and when she tried to control it, her lips began to quiver. Steve snorted gleefully, and Sunny felt the tremblings of hysteria. An instant later, she was struggling to swallow back a paroxysm of giggles. Steve's triumphant bleats and brays undid her. Chortling insanely, she collapsed on the sofa, gasping, crying, helpless.

Several moments passed before she could talk. "You want joy, you'll get joy," she promised, feeling her spirit rally. Tears misted her eyes. She couldn't let him down; she couldn't let any of them down.

All this silliness about Graham Chance was simply that—silliness. She would find a way to rise above it as she had every other obstacle in her life. Not, of course, that there'd been that many, she admitted. And certainly nothing to prepare her for this . . . but let the so-called psychologist do his worst. Chance's intimate observations may have caught her off guard once—well, twice—but she was ready for him now. Let him fire away with those probing looks and questions. She would simply ignore him, drive him crazy with her implacability.

"Okay, business as usual," she resolved firmly, nodding at her producer. She would smile as only Sunny Tyler could smile. And she'd laugh, darn it; she'd be a good sport for Steve's sake, for the staff . . . *for KRBC*.

Sunny's intentions were nothing if not honorable. Despite a sleepless night, she gave it her all the next morning—oh, did she ever. Her smile stretched until it threatened to tickle her ears. Her laughter came precisely on cue, if a trifle shrill, and her energy level, fueled by nerves, soared higher than ever.

Surprisingly, her co-host was cooperative. Chance fed her lines and smoothed out her jerky segues. But despite all his help, she knew she was far from her naturally effervescent self. She felt stiff and artificial, and from the look on Steve Freedkin's face, it showed.

As the last segment ended and the closing theme began, Sunny didn't have to look at the faces of the crew to know the show had flopped again. She'd let them down. Blanchard would never consider them for network airing after two consecutive disasters.

Her chin began to tremble. Before anyone could see, she was off the couch and down the hall. Her dressing room was the first place they'd look, she reasoned, running down the corridor to the back parking lot exit instead.

As she headed toward her car, she could hear sprinting footsteps from behind. A hand caught her and jerked her in the other direction. "You're coming with me," Gray said.

The force of his lead gave her no choice. She either followed him or was dragged. "I guess you're angry, right?" she asked, struggling to keep up. "I don't suppose you've given much thought to the consequences of premeditated violence. Even with the insanity defense, you'd get years—"

"You're tempting me," he muttered, leading her to a red Alfa Romeo and opening the door on the passenger side. "But crisis intervention is more what I had in mind."

He put her into the car.

"Shouldn't that sound more reassuring?" she wondered aloud, wincing as the door banged shut and Chance strode around to the other side. As he slid in beside her, she sensed the taut control that held his frustration in check. "Was I that bad?" she asked quietly.

"Worse," he said. "You were better yesterday when you grabbed the candy and ran. Today you were forced, phony. You were so bad, you made my teeth ache."

"Hey—I was trying," she argued. "Don't I get a little credit for that?" Did he have any idea how hard it was for her to show up this morning, to face the cameras after yesterday's foolishness? "Breaking the rules might be child's play to you, but I'm new at it." Excuses tumbled forth. "Besides, I didn't get much sleep last night, and I'm not used to this new format or to you."

"I'm going to solve that last problem for you." Flicking on the ignition, he backed the Alfa Romeo out, roared past the guard house and onto the street. He slowed to a stop at the corner light and, still looking straight ahead, said, "By the time this day's over you'll be used to me."

She didn't like the sound of that. She didn't want to get used to Graham Chance, not now, not ever. He'd made scrambled eggs of her professional and emotional life. She'd work with him if she had to, but something told her that if she let this man into her personal life in any way, if she let him get too close, she'd never be the same again... A shiver moved through her body and thinned out her voice. "Where are we going?"

"Somewhere we won't be recognized, where they won't even care who we are."

He turned east off the main thoroughfare and drove for several blocks, then traveled north for several more. He's heading into a rough section of town, she realized nervously. The locals might not know or care who Graham Chance and Sunny Tyler were, but that wouldn't stop them from mugging a couple of prosperous-looking Yuppies.

She looked at her blue-eyed abductor. Even a myopic mugger wouldn't mistake this man for an easy mark in his present state of mind, she realized. Gray looked as though he could take on the Marines and win. Her relief was mixed.

She might not be in danger from thugs but was she safe from him?

His jaw muscles jutted, working as he drove. Fascinated, she noticed a slight nick in the blunt angle of jawline that tapered to his chin, a tiny fault line on skin tanned to rich earth hues. She idly wondered if he'd cut himself shaving.

He's rather stunning from this angle, she thought, intrigued by his profile. His features smoldered with character, inbred style and wonderfully aggressive lines.

As his jaw muscles flexed again, an extra breath slipped into the normal rhythm of her respiration. Layers of golden-brown hair dropped on his forehead and swept back over his ears. Umm, nice ears, she noted, grinning a little absurdly.

He pulled the Alfa Romeo over in front of a small shabby bar called Bottoms Up.

"What are we going to do here?" she asked apprehensively.

Without answering, he let her out of the car and lead her toward the entrance. "We're going to come to an understanding, Sunny, one way or the other."

"But why *here*?"

He pulled her along. "No special reason. I picked this place at random because I want a neutral location. Wherever we talk has to be foreign territory to both of us, no psychological advantages."

"Like the SALT talks in Geneva?"

He almost smiled. "Something like that."

The dimly-lit cocktail lounge had a smattering of customers at the bar, a roomful of empty tables and a small dance floor. A scratchy music system was playing a local FM station. Gray picked a table in the corner farthest from the bar. "Something to drink?"

"Perrier?"

He nodded, headed for the bar and came back with two glasses and a pitcher of margaritas. "A little alcohol loosens the tongue and the inhibitions," he explained, filling both glasses. He pushed one toward her, a twinkle in his eye. "Have some truth serum."

She glanced at her watch. "It's not even noon yet."

"It's never too early for honesty." He brushed some salt from the rim of his glass and took a swallow. "Umm. This guy knows his way around a margarita mix."

She laughed and tasted her drink. Surprisingly, it was tangy and delicious. Her tightly strung nerves loosened a notch.

The lounge's dusky ambience and Gray's subtle change of mood had an oddly relaxing effect on her. She felt safe in this murky roadside hideaway, as though they were closeted away from the harsh world outside.

"Okay, enough small talk," he said quietly. "Let's find out why we're setting each other's teeth on edge."

"That's easy," she said sincerely. "You have this knack for making the most upsetting observations. They're just too—" she searched for the right word "—intimate."

To her surprise he nodded in agreement. "I know. I can't seem to resist it where you're concerned. You're such a classic case—"

"Of what?"

His eyes met hers, stirring odd feelings within her. "You just told me you didn't want any more intimate observations."

"Yes, but—"

He touched her hand with long, well-tended fingers. "Someday when you're not afraid of the answer, you'll ask me again. Let's leave it until then."

The simple gesture impaired her breathing. Nodding, she pulled her hand back and began to nurse her drink. The ease with which he read her private thoughts and feelings disturbed her deeply, yet she felt a compelling desire to know everything he saw in her. Don't press, she warned herself, not now that he's agreed to back off.

She looked up again to see him watching her intently.

"Square two," he said. "We've made some headway with your problem, Sunny, now we've got mine to deal with." A smile played about his lips. "Let's see if we can figure out why you set my teeth on edge."

Her heart beat faster. "I didn't know I did."

The smile reached his eyes. "You knew. We both knew, and after this morning there's not a doubt in my mind. The rest of the world might think we're enemies, but you and I know there's an attraction between us that's playing havoc with our ability to work together." He brushed her fingertips with his own. "If we're going to make it professionally, Sunny, we've got to come to terms with *us*."

Sunny felt her stomach tightening into knots again. She wasn't ready to acknowledge an attraction to him, even to herself, but he left her no choice. "Apparently, you're more sure of your feelings than I am—"

"Sunny," he cut in emphatically, "do you want the show to work or not?"

"Of course, I do," she insisted. She wanted it to be the truth, but little swirls of confusion clouded her focus. An answer that should have been so simple suddenly seemed so complicated. There was Ted, her parents, Steve...so many conflicting needs to consider, she'd lost track of what *she* needed. Or rather, what she wanted. What *did* she want?

"Back to square one," he said, taking her hand. "We can't get anywhere here until you're sure about the show. If you want to be there, we've got something to talk about, if you don't..."

"I want the show," she said, nodding. "I do."

His hand tightened around hers. "Good."

They were both quiet then, a moment for coming to grips with the implications of their uneasy alliance.

Gray ended the silence by pouring them both another margarita and holding up his glass. "Let's make it work?"

Sunny exhaled the word, "Yes," and touched her glass to his. She smiled bravely, but inside she sensed she was poised on a threshold...and once she stepped across she could never go back.

They both took a drink, their eyes meeting over the rims of the glasses.

"Now we're back to me," he reminded. "Square two again—my problem with you."

She laughed, trying to cover her growing anxiety. "You're crazy about me, right?"

His eyes glinted, and a golden eyebrow lifted. "Well that may be true, but it's not the problem."

She set her drink down. "What is?"

"You're another man's woman."

"I am?" she questioned. "Oh, of course, Ted."

He laughed out loud, a rich male sound. "Freud must be sitting up in his grave."

"I didn't forget Ted," she said defensively. "It's just the way you say things. I get confused."

"Oh God, you're wonderful," he murmured, still laughing. "You may be confused now, but sooner or later you'll get it figured out. When you do, I hope the free world is ready."

Sunny felt a flush climb her throat.

A melodious ballad came over the stereo system and Gray took her hand. "That's one of my favorites. Let's dance."

"What? Here? It's not even—"

"Noon," he finished for her. "The best possible time for margaritas, honesty...and dancing." His blue eyes met hers with such startling clarity she lost a heartbeat. "I want to dance, Sunny, here, now, with you."

"But you said—I mean—you did say I was another man's woman."

"I asked you to dance, not to marry me. If that's a threat to your commitment to Ted, maybe—"

"It's not," she broke in. "Dancing isn't the problem." Her voice softened, husky, barely audible. "It's...well, it's...you."

His eyes darkened to sparkling lights. Without a word, he came around the table and took her arm.

"Didn't you hear me?" she asked, following his lead to the small parquet dance floor.

Turning her to him, he placed his hands on her shoulders. "I know you belong to someone else, Sunny, and I know I'm not supposed to talk to you intimately, but just for this brief space in time, in this dark little bar, I want to hold you, dance with you."

Her heart beating erratically, she accepted the pull of his hands. An arm slipped behind her shoulder blades and drew her close. His hand captured hers, their fingers automatically interlacing. Looking up at him briefly, she met his eyes and lowered her own, feathery lashes caressing her cheeks.

As the slow strains of the love song floated around them, Sunny followed Gray's lead, so aware of her hand resting on his firmly muscled shoulder, so aware of his nearness . . . of the brushings of their bodies as they moved. Lightly, fleetingly, here and there, they touched and every touch made her pulse rocket.

The music wooed Sunny with its tender lyrics, coaxing up unfamiliar feelings that were warm and vibrant. She closed her eyes, lulled by eddies of soft sensation, gradually losing track of time and her surroundings.

Gray's arms urged her closer and she acquiesced, letting her body arch into full contact with his. A melting sensation weakened her legs, making her step out of time and hit his moving foot. He caught her, wrapped her closer and whispered, "Sorry."

Pressing up against him, the tweedy fiber of his sports jacket abraded and aroused the soft skin exposed by her blouse's low neckline. The scent of his after-shave whirled around them as they swayed, unmindful now of the music, compelled by their own rhythms.

Her cheek just reached his jawline and she let herself nestle against it, remembering his words... *just for this brief space of time I want to hold you....*

Suddenly she realized they'd stopped dancing. She sensed a roughened gentleness in him as he held her away a little. "Do you know what I think, Sunny?"

The look in his eyes warned her, but she had to know. "Tell me, please."

"I think Sunny Tyler's about to discover what she wants—" he hesitated, his eyes deepening their quest "—for the first time. I think she's in the midst of an identity crisis, a rebellion left over from adolescence." His hand coaxed stray tendrils of hair back from her temple. "One she might have had half her life ago if she hadn't been so busy living up to everyone else's expectations. Am I right?"

Inexplicably, her eyelids misted. Lowering them, she answered, "Probably."

His fingers framed her face, lifting it to his. "You lost touch with yourself, and now you're trying to come home. Do it, Sunny. Ask the hard questions, take the risks—"

"Gray, I—" He pressed long fingers to her lips.

"Just one more thing. I won't go after another man's woman, Sunny—but I'm not at all sure you are someone else's. I don't know what you want right now any more than you do, but I'll bet my next paycheck it's not Ted Walsh."

A tiny alarm shrilled inside her. "Ted and I've gone together since high school—"

He nodded. "That's a long time, a solid investment, but is that what you want, what you need from a man? How does it feel when he holds you, when he kisses you, Sunny?" His fingers exquisitely light, he brushed her mouth, lingering, playing with thrilling slowness over the fullness of her lower lip before tracing to her chin and lifting it.

She met his eyes and her body locked, perfectly rigid.

"Like this?" he breathed. His mouth touched hers lightly, vibrantly, dizzying in its gentle assault. As his tongue darted along the seam of her lips, playing at penetration, promising forbidden sensations, Sunny felt a shock wave all the way to her toes. She backed away, her fingers flying to her lips.

"Does he kiss you like that?" Chance asked softly.

Four

Sunny's mouth dropped open. A panicked whisper emerged. "You want me to wear *that*?"

"What's wrong with it?" Steve dangled the pink wisp of spandex from one finger. "It's a leotard for the massage segment. You've never worn a leotard before?"

"*One* of my leotards would make ten of that thing," she protested, still unable to manage more than a whisper. "Just look at it."

Steve held it up to himself and studied the effect. The tiny piece of hot-pink stretch material looked like a New Wave tie. Not only that, he had it upside down. "What's this?" he asked, eyeing an opening.

"It's the newest thing in leg cuts," she said, a wry smile beginning. "Slashed to the armpits. Even if I agreed to wear it—which I haven't—it would never get past the censors."

"What censors?" he said innocently, shooting her a vaudevillian wink. "We're live, remember." He turned it right side up. "Well...what do you think? Another color maybe?"

A comeback just slipped out. "I think pink is perfect with your coloring." *Darn if she wasn't getting pretty good at this repartee stuff.* "And beefcake is so trendy right now."

A grin flickering, Steve sighed in exasperation and tossed the leotard on the couch. "What's the problem?" he said, lifting his shoulders. "All you have to do is wear it under your jump suit through the astrology segment. When we go to break, you'll take off the jump suit, get up on the massage table. You'll be covered with towels—"

"The problem, Steve," she cut in firmly, "is that you keep springing things on me. Co-hosts, leotards—"

"Come on, Sunny." He raised his arms coaxingly. "The show needs something provocative. You know—something outrageous to get those ratings climbing."

"In that case let's have Gray wear it," she deadpanned.

Steve's groan brought a twinge of guilt. Sunny knew how desperate he was to make the show work. She was too, for that matter. Since the agreement with Gray in that dark little bar two weeks before, she'd thrown herself into her roll as co-host with dogged enthusiasm.

Steve retrieved the leotard and waggled it at her.

Still, there were limits to her devotion. "Out of the question," she said firmly, then turned to glance at her makeup mirror. Never mind legions of viewers, the thought of wearing that pink piece of lint in front of Graham Chance sent her heart on a carnival ride. "Besides," she mumbled, "I think I'm coming down with a cold." She sniffled to prove it.

Behind her, Steve sighed resignedly.

Was he giving up? Sunny studied her surprised face. It was getting almost easy to say no to Steve. Could this be the rebellion Gray had predicted? If so, she liked the feel of it.

Now if she could only manage a little rebellion where Chance himself was concerned. Why did her chutzpah lock itself in the closet the instant she encountered his unreasonably blue eyes? And that smile, so wonderfully slow and seductive it suggested the unthinkable.... A warm shiver moved down her spine.

Steve's reflection, narrow and shrewd, appeared above her own. "Is this the same cold that kept you from modeling the negligees last week, or is this a brand-new bug?" He shook a finger at her. "What's going on, Sunny? Do I detect the sudden onset of girlish self-consciousness? The flutters of sexual awakening? Love's first blush?" A maddening "I gotcha" grin wreathed his thin face.

Color seeped into her cheeks. "Don't be ridiculous."

A frantic tap at the door saved her from further embarrassing denials.

"Five minutes. Get out here!" a voice called.

Steve opened the door and waved her along. "Personally, I think this thing you and Gray've got going is kinda cute," he said, lowering his voice to a conspiratorial hush.

Something in his expression compelled her to try and make him understand. "All right," she whispered as they strode down the hall to the set. "Maybe there is an attraction, but it's completely innocent."

"And I'm an Eagle Scout," he whispered back.

Gray was waiting on the set, relaxed, ready, seated in his co-host position on the couch when they arrived. Sunny tried to work up some animosity for the casual and completely professional way he'd adapted to the new format.

The chaos of last-minute changes, five-minute segments, promos, demos and some very bizarre guests required a spontaneity and lightning-quick reaction time that had kept Sunny constantly on her toes. Between the show and her new co-host, the past two weeks had been an exciting, exhilarating flat-out adrenaline high.

And Gray's behavior had added to the general confusion. *He'd been wonderful.* Helpful and discreet. He'd never again mentioned their interlude in the bar...and wondering why he hadn't was driving her crazy.

On the set, he'd been downright solicitous. Like the time he waited until the break to whisper that the pops and crackles that had the sound men frantic were coming from her own mike. "You're sitting on it," he'd explained. Such mortification.

Sunny shook her head and took a breath, clearing her mind.

Gray glanced up, and she felt sparks running along the connection their eyes made. As an undercurrent of sensuality darkened his features, her own breathing quickened. Were his good intentions wearing thin?

Could the viewers sense it? she wondered, walking up to join him on the couch. Did everybody see the electricity she felt whenever she entered Graham Chance's territory? Little bubbles of nervous laughter threatened to break through her cool smile.

"Morning, Gray," she said, aware of the lilt in her voice.

As he nodded and blessed her with an incredible smile, a tiny crease appeared in his cheek. Darn, *that's* sexy, she admitted, surprised she hadn't noticed it before.

"Ready to have your stars charted?" he asked, indicating their first guest, a popular astrologist waiting off camera with Steve.

"I'm a Gemini," she said, wondering why in the world she'd said it. Something, thank God, kept her from asking him what his sign was.

"Maybe you'd better sit down," Gray suggested. "We're thirty seconds to air."

She sat. But not before fastening her microphone firmly on her lapel.

The first segment went surprisingly well. After informing Gray and Sunny that their show had "marvelous aspects," the effusive redheaded astrologer spent the remainder of the segment advising star-crossed call-in viewers on love and life.

Sunny handled herself admirably. With acute concentration, she trained eyes, ears—and a mind that wanted to stray to the muscled leg brushing hers—on the astrologer's predictions.

At the break, she quickly leafed through, *The Secrets of Sensual Massage*, their next guest's book. One look at the illustrations told her that refusing to wear the pink leotard had been an act of unparalleled wisdom on her part.

She shut the book as Gray leaned over to take a peek.

"I bought a copy for my coffee table," he said, disconcerting her with a roguish wink.

Gray introduced their next guest with a flourish. "Okay, let's bring out the lady we've all been waiting for, Helga Clemp, the author of the best-selling, do-it-yourself massage manual."

A large-boned blonde strode onto the set. Nearly six feet tall, she spoke in a husky accent of undetermined origins. "I write book for da body, da muscles, da mind," she said, giving Gray's hand a vigorous shake.

"Yes, you certainly did," Sunny agreed brightly. She held the book up to the camera as Helga sat down. "And I understand you're a licensed masseuse. Do you find that to be satisfying work?"

"I loff my vork," Helga said briskly. She flexed her impressive hands. "Shall I give massage?"

Sunny shook her head. "No, no massages today, thank you. Let's just discuss your book—"

"I vant give massage," she insisted, looking straight at Graham. "I vork on him."

"Me?" Smiling, Gray pointed to himself. He shot Sunny a skeptical look. "Weren't you supposed to do the massage demo?"

At Sunny's sort of shrug, Gray glanced at the assistant producer. He sort of shrugged, too.

Gray shook his head pleasantly, resisting the masseuse's determined stare. "Sorry, I'm not dressed for it."

A wicked idea crossed Sunny's mind. "Nonsense, he'd love to be... vorked on," she said impulsively.

The woman's eyes glowed. She flexed her hands again. "Vhatever's vrong vit you," she promised Gray, "I fix it."

Gray hit Sunny with a brief "get you later" glare. "Can you fix a broken neck?" he asked Helga, smiling thinly.

"Sure," Helga said, nodding. "I'm good vit necks."

"We have to take a short break now," Sunny cut in, smiling at the camera. "But stay tuned. When we come back, Helga will demonstrate her techniques of sensual massage—right after she fixes Gray's neck."

As the light blinked off, Sunny grabbed her copy of Helga's book and headed for the portable massage table waiting on a small adjacent demo set. With a grateful sigh, she heard Helga block Gray's pursuit with a detailed account of her therapeutic plans for him.

Sunny averted her eyes from Gray's glare as they arrived.

"Remoff your clothes und get on table," Helga instructed Gray, rolling up her sleeves.

Gray blanched. The floor manager flashed a "no go" signal. Steve's voice from the booth overruled them both. "Go ahead, Gray. Take off your jacket and shirt. It'll be great for ratings."

Sunny squelched a giggle. Her co-host looked ready to commit mayhem as he jerked off his jacket, loosened his tie and began to unbutton his shirt with slow deliberate hands.

She watched with discreet fascination as Gray's shirt fell open, revealing a prominent collarbone and pectorals gracefully textured with muscle definition and whorls of golden-brown hair. As he pulled the shirt free of his pants, she felt a distinct need to swallow—and did, a near gulp.

His tanned upper torso glistened with subtle strength under the harsh studio lights. Sunlightened chest hair swirled over muscle and dipped down to his navel. Biceps flexing, he tossed the shirt and tie over a nearby chair.

Sunny's fingers tingled. Her heartbeat went light and high as she became aware of an impossible desire to touch the contracted muscle of his arm. Her hands closed to fists, and a slight tremor brought a soft sound of surprise. Gray looked up sharply, and she forced her expression to one of professional disinterest.

Who was she kidding? Not him certainly. His eyes touched her briefly, and their narrowing brightness told her he suspected her secret wish. Sunny looked away, allowing herself an instant to speculate on his desires. Did the thought of her cool fingers on his skin do crazy things to his stomach, too?

She forced her attention to the masseuse as the floor manager signaled the end of the break and the show's theme music began.

Helga busied herself setting up, pulling towels and containers of scented oils from a small suitcase. "Ready," she said as Gray swung himself onto the massage table and lay on his stomach.

Sunny felt an inner twitch as she watched him fold his arms under his head. Triceps rippled and a wave of energy traveled down his spine as muscles relaxed. Heaven help us all, she thought, taking a deep breath, he's dangerous at any angle. Why hadn't Ted's back ever affected her this way?

The camera light flashed on unexpectedly. She hadn't even heard the countdown. "Oh, we're back," she ad-libbed lamely. "All ready to demonstrate the massage? Helga? Gray?" she asked.

"Ready," Helga said in a voice that rivaled a drumroll. "First, ve must use plenty of varm oil," she explained, making enthusiastic swipes up and down Gray's back until he fairly glistened.

"Okay, dat's good," she said finally. Standing back, she gave his back a healthy slap.

Gray grunted.

"Be gentle, Helga," Sunny advised, glad her co-host was immobilized. If she were smart, she'd make a fast exit from this set before the masseuse let him up.

"Now I vork da tension from his muscles," Helga said, nodding at the camera. She gave Gray another good-natured thwack. "After dat I demonstrate sensual massage."

Her large hands began to knead his shoulder muscles, massaging in deep simultaneous circles. Gray let out a soft groan as she worked down his back. Pain or pleasure? Sunny wondered, smiling apprehensively. She shrugged at the camera. "Isn't it refreshing to watch a woman who loves her work?"

Frowning, Helga thumped up and down Gray's back with brisk karatelike chops. "Got too much tension," she muttered.

"Maybe if you stopped hitting him," Sunny suggested.

The masseuse shook her head with conviction. "Gotta show muscles who's da boss." After several more rolling chops, she announced, "Now Helga needs get up on table."

Sunny's eyes widened as the masseuse actually hoisted herself up onto the table and pursued the tension in Gray's back with unbridled vigor. She slapped and tickled and did a series of knuckle-thumping drill across his shoulders.

The floor manager waved wildly, directing the camera in for a better angle on the action.

Without losing a beat, Helga narrated her assault with a running commentary on her techniques. "Good, yeah?" she asked Gray.

"What the hell is she doing?" he grated.

Sunny was too stunned to intervene. The crew whooped with laughter.

"Tension all gone, yeah?" Helga inquired, thumbs and fingers alternately smoothing and digging into muscle mass.

A nervous giggle escaped through Sunny's astonishment. "Excuse me, Helga," she hazarded, "but I'm sure there's a clause in our insurance coverage that prohibits two on a massage table."

Up in the booth, Steve flashed a thumbs-up sign. His grin nearly cracked the glass. He loves a good spectacle, Sunny thought ironically. No use counting on him for any help in getting this dynamo off her co-host.

"That's enough, Helga," she said firmly.

The masseuse looked around at Sunny and smiled. "I vorking good now," she said. "I fix his neck."

"Like hell," Gray muttered, lifting up.

"Helga—" Sunny forced some menace into her voice "—*that's enough.*"

The masseuse registered sincere surprise. "You vant stop?" She gave Gray's back another quick round of knuckling and swung off the table. Grabbing a towel for her oily hands, she beamed at him with obvious pride. "All better, yeah?"

Gray managed a pained smile. "Terrific."

She turned to Sunny. "You try it now?"

"Try what?" Sunny said warily.

"Massage." Helga grinned and winked. "I show you da sensual method?"

"Sounds good to me," Gray said, brightening.

"We're almost out of time," Sunny protested, ignoring the floor manager's "keep rolling" signals.

"Nonsense, we've got plenty of time," said Gray, obviously enjoying himself.

Helga handed Sunny a scented squeeze bottle. "Oil hands."

Propped on one elbow, Gray's mouth quirked into a contagious grin as he watched Sunny grimace and then gingerly squeeze oil on her palms.

"Be careful," Sunny muttered, looking down her nose at him, "or these hands will have you begging for mercy."

"Promise?" he asked, his voice husky.

The crew's laughter quieted to titters as they waited expectantly. The cameras moved in. A hush swept across the set.

Settling his head into the cradle of his arms, Gray closed his eyes and anticipated the touch of his co-host's fingers. He willed his muscles to relax.

"Start here," he heard Helga direct, administering another friendly thump to his lower back. "Den move hands up...."

Gray tuned out the masseuse's instructions, and an instant later he felt cool palms make contact with the small of his back. The pressure was light, almost fluttery. The fingers felt long and tapered. Sunny's hands.

His muscles tensed despite his efforts to keep them relaxed. Her hands moved slowly up his back, thumbs riding gently along the ridges on either side of his spine. Spread out like butterfly wings, her fingers trembled slightly.

"Am I doing it right?" he heard her ask Helga. The slight tremor in her voice made his jaw draw tight.

"Yeah," Helga said enthusiastically, continuing her ongoing lecture on the endless benefits of massage.

The masseuse's voice drifted out of focus, becoming a background drone as Gray's attention fixated on the hands that caressed his back. Fingertips purled up along his shoulder blades, gliding over them and down to curl around his biceps.

His stomach muscles pulled taut. Peripherally aware of the camera moving in for a close-up, he quickly rolled his head to the other side.

"Am I doing it right?" Sunny asked again. Her voice sounded far away, as faint as a quivery harp chord.

Right? He couldn't ever remember hands feeling so right before.

Her fingers slipped over into the hollows between his shoulders and collarbone, dipping, climbing with the ascending curve, dipping again. They trailed along the cords of his neck, touching around, lingering on the quick movement of his Adam's apple as he swallowed.

Was she *trying* to arouse him? Something grabbed and yanked down low inside him.

An energy seemed to come from her palms and connect with all his vital points like a live current.

Suddenly fingernails scraped softly down his sides to his waist. He swallowed a moan of pleasure, his thigh muscles contracting involuntarily.

A familiar sensation claimed his attention, a spontaneous flickering of life in his loins. Damn, he realized, if she doesn't cut that out . . .

He held his breath and willed his responses back under control.

Helga's voice broke through. "I tink he liking dis massage, yeah?"

Sunny didn't answer. Her knuckles inched along the small of his back, applying and releasing pressure. Her hands made claws, rippling up and down in continuous waves. *Her fingertips played along his belt line.*

Featherlike, quivering touches betrayed her arousal, and Gray absorbed their sheer excitement.

"Enough?" Sunny asked Helga, her voice unsteady.

Enough, he shouted silently. Heat pulsed through him. He groaned inwardly. *It's too late now.*

"Yeah," Helga agreed. "Now ve turn him over, do his chest."

A pleading note crept into Sunny's voice. "Is that really necessary?"

Turn over? Managing a smile, Gray lifted up on his forearms. "I'd rather not do that." Turning away from the cameras, he shot Sunny a warning glare.

"Vhat?" the masseuse exclaimed. "But ve only haf done."

"Trust me," he said, his eyes still fixed on Sunny. "You've done more than enough already."

Awareness sharpened Sunny's features. A splotch of crimson climbed up her neck. She smiled at the cameras. "We're going to have to skip the rest of this terrific massage demonstration because Graham has a cramp in his leg, right, Gray?"

He nodded at Sunny, one eye on the camera mercilessly closing in. "That's right, Sunny. In fact, maybe you'd better go on over and begin the interview with our next guest, Maria Collins, the soaps' favorite villainess. I'll join you afterward for the ESP segment."

Sunny nodded, then remembered Helga. Starting to offer the woman her oily hand, she instantly pulled it back and wiped it on the nearest blotter, Gray's slacks.

The crew gasped out a chuckle. Gray mumbled what would probably have qualified as an obscenity violation under his breath.

Startled, Sunny jerked the still-oily hand away. "Helga," she gushed, covering, "it's been a pleasure. You certainly know your stuff."

Flashing the camera a dazzling smile, Sunny picked up Helga's book. "*The Secrets of Sensual Massage*, folks. It's all here and it works."

The red light blinked off.

"And if you don't believe me, ask my co-host," she murmured. A flushed smile appeared as she offered Gray a large towel and then hurried off the set.

Sunny took one last hurried sip of coffee, set the cup in the kitchen sink and grabbed her purse and keys. A supermarket tabloid lay on the Formica dinette table, it's headline glaring up at her "Talk Show Hosts—Secret Romance!"

She quickly folded and tucked it into her purse along with copies of the other gossip rags that had cropped up in the past week, all with similar headlines.

The telephone rang just as she reached her apartment door. Damn, she swore silently. She *had* to get to work early today and talk with Steve about these scandal sheets.

"Let it ring," she said, her hand on the doorknob.

But the insistent bleating demanded her attention, and she whirled around to pick it up.

"Sunny!" someone called even before she had the receiver to her ear.

The voice sounded high, kind of screechy. "Ted?"

"I've been trying to get you all week," he barked. "Where have you been?"

"Busy," she told him. "It's the new format. We're booking twice as many guests, there's more prep time and rehearsal. I've got bios and books to read—"

"Never mind," he cut in. "Have you seen this week's *Midnight Inquirer*?"

She looked at her stuffed purse. "Yes, as a matter of fact, I—"

"What the hell does this headline mean, Sunny? A secret romance? And the cover— He's got his shirt off, and you— my God!—you're clawing at his back. Inside there's a shot of you having dinner with him. *What's going on?*"

"If you'd let me finish," she countered, "I'll tell you." Where was the sweet gentle Ted she'd agreed to marry? Had politics created this insensitive autocrat?

"The cover picture is from the show," she explained, "a perfectly innocent massage segment we did last week. The dinner was lunch—*a working lunch*. Steve was there, too, but the paparazzi cut him out of the picture."

"Paparazzi," he moaned. "My God, Sunny, this can't go on."

"I know, Ted, I know," she soothed. "I'm on my way to work right now. I've got the tabloids and I'm going to talk to Steve. We'll figure something out."

"If you don't, Sunny, I swear I'm coming out there again—"

"Gotta go, Ted," she said. "Don't worry, now. I'll take care of everything." She hung up the phone, took a deep breath and left.

It wasn't until she'd pulled her Karman Ghia onto the freeway that she realized she hadn't told Ted she loved him.

Reporters awaited her at KRBC's gates. They were staked out along the road with flashbulbs and minicams, Gray's former station among them.

As she lowered the window a crack and slowed to enter the lot, they stormed the car, thrusting microphones and questions at her. Several of them held up the *Midnight Inquirer* and the other tabloids.

"Lies, all lies," she said dramatically. "Not a word of truth in any of those stories." They rushed to scribble down her statement. Good, she thought, maybe Ted would calm down when her denial hit the papers.

Refusing further questions, she pulled through the gates, parked and hurried toward her dressing room. Surprised to find the door slightly ajar, she was even more startled to find both Steve and Gray waiting inside.

Her producer looked about to explode with contained energy. And something distinctly dangerous crackled in her co-host's watchful eyes.

It had to be the scandal sheets. "I'm glad you're both here," she said, pulling the papers from her purse. "You've seen these, of course, and the reporters outside."

Steve nodded, declining to take the tabloids.

Sunny felt her heartbeat quicken at the look on Gray's face. Why was he studying her so intently? She felt like a window being measured for drapes.

"Why don't you sit down, Sunny," he suggested. "Steve has some news." A certain movement had slipped into Gray's voice. A low timbre edged the words with expectancy.

She sat, clasping her purse and the tabloids tighter.

Steve began to pace, his energy spilling out all over the room. "We've done it, Sunny!" he blurted. "I kept it quiet because I didn't want to make you nervous. Sometimes success can be stressful. I thought maybe the pressure—"

"Done *what*?"

"The latest ratings," Gray interjected. "They're pretty impressive."

"Impressive?" Steve wailed. "They're mind-boggling! We're peaking out. Our overnight's broke the show's all-time high. If this keeps up, they'll be orbiting the earth!"

Sunny knew the numbers were good, but she had no idea....

"Listen—it gets better," Steve said, dropping to his knees in front of her chair. "The studio brass came through! Now that we're hot, they're going to back my idea." He bounced back up with a triumphant whoop. Too overcome with his good fortune to share it coherently, he paced, laughed, slapped his head.

"What idea?" Sunny asked faintly.

"They've agreed to shoot the show on location," Gray explained, a subtle current moving beneath the blue of his eyes.

"Location? Where? When? How long?"

"Next week," Steve tossed out between whoops.

"Las Vegas," Gray added. "We'll be there seven days." Stretching an arm along the back of the couch, he smiled. He looked like a man who'd just won a weekend with Christie Brinkley.

Sunny's throat went dry. Seven days in Sin City with this man and his motel smile? "How can we go to Las Vegas?"

she protested hoarsely. "When the papers are already full of lies and scandal about us."

"Oh gawd," Steve crooned. "Lies, scandal. I love it!"

"Listen," she said, dead serious now. "We've got to stop these stories. Ted's—"

The producer lifted her up out of the chair and hugged her breathless. "We will, Sunny, we will stop them...later." Planting a big kiss on her nose, he grabbed her shoulders, held her away and looked straight into her eyes. It was hard not to smile at the absurd grin wreathing his features and the huge glasses sliding down his nose.

"This is it, Sunny. Blanchard's man called me last night. If we can keep the numbers up, we're in! He practically promised Blanchard would pick us for the network." He shook her wildly. "This is it, Sunshine. Glitz and glory time! For you, me, Gray, the entire crew! *My mother in Miami!* Do you know how long she's waited for her son the producer to make it big? She'll be able to watch *my* show on her portable Sony!"

Steve babbled on, but Sunny couldn't hear him. *Picked up for the network?* In the midst of her euphoria, another image rippled across her mind like wind through a field of wheat. Seven days in Las Vegas with Graham Chance...? Her lower eyelid began to quiver and her fingers flew to the spot.

From his chair, Gray sat quietly watching, his eyes trained on her the way a cat observes a bird about to land.

Five

———

Tossing restlessly in the king size bed, Sunny rolled to her back and stared up at the ceiling. "Go to sleep," she muttered softly. But her mind remained obstinately alert.

Las Vegas was at its mild desert best in April; her room at the MGM Grand was sumptuous; the "live-on-location" shows had run beautifully all week. Everything was going so well. So why this persistent feeling of disquiet?

Ted's churlish phone calls disturbed her, of course. If he wasn't pressuring her to marry him, he was frantic over some new headline. When her denials of a romance to the press resulted in more lurid stories, he'd called from his Washington office, furious. "For God's sakes, use your head, Sunny," he'd ranted. "From now on it's *no comment* to those scavengers. Is that clear?"

"No comment," she'd mumbled and hung up the phone.

When he called back, they'd had their first real fight in fifteen years. Finally, in a plea for peace, she agreed to stonewall the press if he'd stop pressuring her to marry him.

"Ted, listen to me," she soothed. "Maybe we both need a breather, some unpressured time to—"

"You've had enough *time*, Sunny," Ted bit back, obviously infuriated by her suggestion. "I want to set a date for the wedding. Set a date or I'll—"

"Don't give me an ultimatum, Ted," she warned quietly. "If you give me an ultimatum I'll hang up—*again*."

"If you hang up again I'm coming to Las Veg—"

The phone receiver phone hit the cradle. And Ted hadn't called back since....

Sunny shut her eyes. Had she really known Ted for fifteen years? For half her life? He seemed so remote now, a virtual stranger. Had he changed? Or had she?

It's Ted, she decided, rolling to her side. He'd become so proprietary, almost parental. Every move she made seemed to upset him, even her efforts to help. "Your image is as important as mine, Sunny," he warned continually. "A congressman's wife is a demanding role." He made her feel like an auditioning actress who might not get the part.

She threw back the sheets, slipped out of bed and walked to the window of her fifth-floor room overlooking the pool.

As she gazed down through the soft-lit darkness at the glittering water, the cabana bars and the wandering couples with drinks in their hands, a sigh slipped out. She wanted to be down there, too, laughing, drinking, staying up late. She was tired of hiding out in this room each night, avoiding the press, avoiding Gray—and all for Ted's sake. She was tired of auditioning.

It came to her all in a rush. She didn't want the part. Her breath caught. She didn't want to play Mrs. United States Congressman. *She didn't want to marry Ted Walsh.* The realization seemed so chillingly final a shiver ran down her arms. She hugged herself and closed her eyes.

Dear God, after fifteen years. How would Ted react? What would her parents think?

She hugged herself tighter, letting out a low, head shaking groan. Was jilting a congressman treason? She winced as a stab of guilt brought her up short. She couldn't hurt Ted, her parents—the three people she cared most about in this world.

Grimacing, eyes squeezing shut, she felt her stomach churn with conflict. After several tense moments, she opened them slowly...and knew the truth. She couldn't marry Ted, not now, not feeling as she did.

The awareness came gradually. It's not Ted, she realized, *it's me*. I've changed. She wasn't quite sure how, or why, but in that moment, she knew she could never be the kind of wife a congressman needed. Something had happened, *was happening* inside her, something wonderful, inexplicable. And whatever it was, it demanded that she discover the feelings that had been building for weeks; feelings that were surging up at this very moment.

Trying to still her tumultuous thoughts, she listened to the soft yearnings within her, listened to the hushed voice of adventure that whispered in her ear. It coaxed her to sample life, take risks, live each day to its full potential.

A vibration of pure excitement, almost frightening, moved through her. She inhaled deeply and moved closer to the window. Her fingers touching the pane, she began to search the pool area. Would she find a blue-eyed man down there among the tourists having a drink? Signing autographs? Had he gone to a show, or stayed alone in his room?

Gambling. she thought, shivering. She pictured Gray gambling—fearlessly, for high stakes—and winning. Underneath the psychologist's man-in-charge persona, Gray had the heart of an adventurer. Risk taking would run in his blood.

She pressed her forehead against the window, painfully aware of how much that part of his persona excited her. "Oh Lord," she groaned, *everything about him excited her.*

Some incredible kind of chemistry was working, and it had made the past week the most anxiety-provoking of her life.

Gray's eyes, his smile, his voice, his accidental touch had become a dangerous trip-wire to her senses.

In her worst moments, his every movement, every murmur tugged at her demanding her attention. During an outdoor sequence, he'd absently brushed wind-ruffled hair from her cheek, a simple gesture, yet for an instant in time nothing could break that urgent connection of skin caressing skin.

Drawing in a long, shaky breath, she eased around, letting her shoulders and the back of her head rest against the window. Did he feel the same way? Did his mind register her every move?

Or was there a much simpler explanation? Adventurers pursued the unattainable. Was that his motivation? Was it hers? Was this wild attraction simply because they couldn't have each other?

She shook herself gently and pulled the curtains shut. "Enough," she whispered. "Get some sleep."

The sheets had grown cool in her absence. She slipped into them with a shivery sigh and threw her arms above her head. Darkness surrounded her. Shutting her eyes, she waited for the chill to soothe the nervous energy from her body and let her rest.

"Another Scotch rocks?" the bartender asked, his voice an unexpected intrusion. Gray shook his head, lost in moody piano chords, clinking glasses, low-pitched voices . . . background music for the clutter of his thoughts.

He nursed his drink a while longer, then swung around on the bar stool. This is ridiculous, he thought surveying the dimly-lit activity in the cocktail lounge. In a town where action, excitement and beautiful women abounded, how had he ended up here? Drinking. Alone.

He had a perfect excuse, of course. To wander out into the lobby or the casinos was to risk a mob scene. The scandal sheets had done their job. Most of the people here had never seen the show, but they knew his well-publicized face.

He swung back around and signaled for another drink. Up in his room, homework for the next day's show waited to be read. He'd tried to review it, but a restlessness had seized him, and he'd walked out.

Now he had a whole night to kill, a clip full of money in his pocket, and no desire to play the tables. He'd even skipped dinner, ignoring the hotel's gourmet restaurants and buffets. Food couldn't begin to satisfy the appetites building inside him.

A slender blonde eased up to the bar. Gray's breath hitched in; his head snapped around. She smiled, inclined her head, then turned to the bartender and ordered a drink.

Lord, for a moment he'd thought it was . . .

His heart thundered like a freight train. That morning's show came flooding back to him. Images he'd been trying to extinguish all day. Sunny, modeling the latest thing in skimpy summer fashions; colorful sun outfits, clinging one-piece maillots and high-tech bikinis. He'd had trouble catching his breath when she'd sashayed past him; he'd even flushed like an idiot when she'd tossed him a shy playful wink.

His analytical eye had immediately told him she'd lost weight in the past few weeks, probably from nerves. But the effect of her endless legs and the soft bounce of her breasts had unnerved him.

Fresh from poolside lounging, she'd glowed soft, tan and warm as the sunlit morning. He'd had a gut-wrenching desire to swing that lithe body up into his arms.

A chuckle formed as he took a deep, steadying drink of his Scotch. What would the papers have done with that action?

They'd love it, of course. And so would the viewers. They loved everything he and Sunny did—the fluffed intros, the garbled words, even the major screw ups—but what really hooked them was the indefinable energy that charged the air when he and Sunny worked together.

The press had dubbed their style "electric television."

"They're saturating the local airwaves," one prominent reviewer had written, "and the reaction is raising static from coast to coast."

Even their own crew watched them with baited breath, as though they were two live wires about to connect. Was the whole world waiting for something to happen between Sunny Tyler and Graham Chance?

Gray felt a tightening in his stomach as the obvious struck him: nothing would happen unless he made it happen. No matter how Sunny might feel about him, she wouldn't act on it—she *couldn't* act on it as long as she believed herself committed to Ted.

Damn, he thought, exhaling. She's no more committed to Ted than I am. All I need is a little time alone with her. He gripped his glass harder as he thought about how he would touch her, arouse her, make her acknowledge what she really felt.

A painful energy coursed through him. He pushed his drink away and laid a bill on the counter.

As he reached the lounge's door, his conscience momentarily slowed him. What the hell are you doing, Chance? She's taken, engaged to Walsh. You've been through this once before, remember...and people got *hurt*.

But the warning didn't stop him this time.

Sunny sat bolt upright in bed. Had she heard a tap on the door? A tremor ran through her as she listened...and heard it again.

She pulled the covers around her, fighting the urge to crawl under them. You have to answer it, she ordered. It might be Steve, or the show's director.

She slipped on her robe and hurried to the door. "Steve?" she called hopefully.

At the blunt "No, it's Gray" she took a breath, unlatched the door and backed away several feet.

She steadied herself against the dresser as the door swung open. The man on the threshold had a stark, almost driven look in his eyes.

"Gray?" she questioned softly.

He stepped inside and shut the door behind him.

"Gray, you shouldn't be—" Her throat closed painfully, cutting off the words.

She took in his physical appearance in one nervous blink. A navy-and-white rugby shirt, a navy sweater draped around his neck and khaki jeans. He might have walked out of a magazine ad if it weren't for the disorganized mane of golden-brown hair and the stark message in his eyes.

"We have to...talk," he said, his tone edging toward harshness.

She looked down and clutched her robe closed. "Now?"

"Now," he said walking to her. He stopped a foot away, and yet he felt so unnervingly near she could barely breathe.

The space between them vibrated with an almost tangible force.

She averted her gaze, catching her image in the mirror. The wild scatter of her hair startled her. The look in her own darkening eyes disturbed and aroused her. A flashpoint of fear and excitement spiraled up from inside.

Like a needle prick, the tiny inner voice of survival warned her to make him leave. She stiffened, a protest starting to form.

With a touch as definite as a command, he reached over, took hold of her arm and the connection was made. She felt a pulse moving through his fingers that overtook her own frenzied beat and held it throbbing in place.

"Sunny," he said, his voice low, brusque. "I'm here because there's nowhere left for me to run tonight."

His usual resonance was betrayed by an emotion that arrested her.

His hand moved up her arm, hovered at her shoulder. "Sometimes patience is more than a virtue," he said, "sometimes it's expedient. A shrewd man knows when to wait—" His fingers played with the satin nightgown strap that peeked from under her robe. "God knows, I've always considered myself a shrewd man . . ."

There was something choked, almost vulnerable in his voice.

She looked up at him and a soft moan wavered in her throat. His eyes were brilliant and blue; a shimmering energy moved beneath them. His jaw flexed, a nerve drawing the muscles taut.

She watched, fascinated, as his lips parted expectantly, about to say something . . . and then closed, silent.

Compelled to know what he hadn't said, she moved closer.

"Gray?" she queried softly, breathing rapidly, trying to fill the lightness inside her with swallows of air.

He took her other arm, drew her closer. His mouth tried to form a smile. "Sunny—" Warm breath, smoky with liquor, rushed over her face. "I don't like coming here. I don't like what I'm about to do—"

A thrill caught deep inside her, tightening then opening like a flower. Waves of pleasure fanned through her, softening, weakening her limbs. She closed her eyes, afraid to hear him, afraid of the hands that slid up to frame her throat.

"Gray, don't," she said as his thumbs caressed the trembling cords of her neck, then gently pressed up, lifting her chin, forcing her head up.

She kept her eyes squeezed shut.

"Sunny, you don't love Ted Walsh," he said, his voice whisper-harsh near her ear. "You don't want him. I'm so sure of it, I can feel it. And you would too, if you'd just let yourself."

She felt his thumbs curling under the neckline of her robe, felt him easing the silky material away, sliding it over the rise of her shoulders. She breathed in shivery air, exhaling a tremor of release as the robe cascaded to the floor. Her wispy nightgown rustled, caressing bare skin.

Her eyes flickered open, unfocused, infused with her inner conflict. They asked him to stop; they told him not to stop.

"You don't want him, Sunny," he said, his knuckles sliding across her cheek, easing her disarrayed hair back behind her ear with heart-stealing slowness. "I know you don't want him. You know it."

"I...I..." She shook her head, pulled back involuntarily.

His fingers swept up into her hair, working, tangling, gripping the back of her head. His other hand anchored her shoulder.

She felt her world telescope, narrow to sharp pinpoints of light, each flash triggered by the spur of his fingers. In that moment she felt nothing but the strength of those controlling hands.

Suspended, she met his eyes and felt a sensation streak down to her vitals. Her mouth parted spontaneously and a tremorous cry slipped out.

His eyes burned her with their intent. His hand dropped to hers, captured it. He touched her fingers to his mouth, brushing them along the textured softness of his lips. "What is it you want, Sunny?"

Parting his lips slightly, he guided her rigid fingers along their inner moistness. "If it's this," he said, his voice low with emotion, "tell me." His tongue touched the pulse in her fingertips; his teeth captured a tiny section of soft flesh.

She gasped as he bit down gently. Desire shivered and flared. Deep inside her, a twist of pleasure pulled tight.

The hand he'd entangled in her hair closed into a fist and urged her toward him. "Come here," he murmured.

Resistance evaporated in a steamy blur of sensation. Surrendering, she went with the pull of his arms, letting her head be drawn back with the tug of his fist.

His mouth touched her first, hovered at her lips like a bee drawing essence from a flower. Magical fingers feathered along her cheekbones. All at once, she felt such sweetness, such fierce sensuality.

A shared sigh built and breathed out, rushing, eddying within the soft play of their lips. *He whispered things she couldn't hear, wanted to hear.*

Her eyes fluttering shut, she sought him with her hands and found a hard-angled jawline. The beginnings of a heavy beard prickled her skin. Fingertips touched the soft curved lobe of his ear.

With a muted groan, he released her hair. His hand flashed to the small of her back and pulled her up against heat and hard lines of desire.

The full-out contact startled and thrilled her. Her body responded with a tug of stimulation, a deep burst of light, a shuddering sigh.

"Oh, Sunny," he murmured, his mouth brushing, rustling, murmuring over her face. "This is what it's all been about the past few weeks. This is what *we're about*."

She felt him tremble as he eased his mouth onto hers again. Pleasure moved through her like a river. And the deepening pressure of his lips elicited a longing so intense it brought a sweet wrench of pain. Her legs nearly gave way as his arms locked her in a kiss that was long and deep and endless.

"Sunny, Sunny," he rasped, the hunger in his voice tapping into her own, drawing it into sharp focus. "Tell me this is right, that you want me. God, I need to hear you say it."

Emotion stole her voice. With unsteady fingers, she reached up to touch his face, caress his mouth.

Groaning an expletive, he muttered, "I never meant to do this. I'm pushing you too hard, pressuring—"

"I know," she whispered.

His eyes narrowed. He took hold of her arms, held her away. "You know? Does that mean you want me to leave?"

"No," she murmured, "it means I know I don't love Ted. I mean . . . I think I know. I mean I think I don't love him— I mean—oh, God—"

"Do you hear what you're saying?" he said, seizing her tighter.

With a jerky nod, she met his eyes and moved to him spontaneously. He held her, nearly crushed the breath out of her and just as quickly released her.

"Gray," she cautioned, seeing the controlled urgency that glinted from his eyes. His deliberation stunned her to silence as he hooked the strap of her nightgown with an index finger and slipped it off her shoulder.

Her eyes followed his hand as he slowly lowered the other strap. Mesmerized, she watched her nightgown slip down, saw it linger on the flushed rising of her breasts, quivering there briefly before it dropped to the floor.

A small cry caught in her throat.

He swept her up, his arms straining with purpose, and strode to the bed.

Easing her onto the sheets, he gently caressed her face and throat. With one hand, he worked the buttons of his shirt free, growled impatiently, left the shirt half undone and unbuckled his belt. Male urgency radiated around him like a force field.

Watching, she felt a little shock of fear. The delayed realization of what they were about to do suddenly dawned, widening her eyes. Little alarms went off in her head. This is real; this is happening, she thought. He intends to make love to me. Here. *Now.*

A trembling hesitation stiffened her limbs, and she reached for the sheet reflexively, covering her breasts.

He paused, fingers on his belt, a question in his eyes.

"This is too fast, Gray," she breathed. "I—"

The words broke off in a gasp. She sat up, recoiling as the telephone erupted with a harsh shrill.

It rang again. Her eyes went to the receiver, but Gray's hand rose to stay her. "Don't answer it."

She hesitated, paralyzed. "I have to," she whispered. "It might be Steve, or the director calling about tomorrow's show."

"Let it ring," he told her. "They'll call back."

But when the phone shrilled again, she picked it up.

"Sunny?" The familiar voice sent a shock wave through her. *Ted.*

"I'm in the lobby," he muttered under his breath. "The desk clerk won't give me your room number unless you okay it."

"You're here?" she asked, her voice thin with shock. "What are you doing *here*?"

"I just flew in from Washington. Now listen to me, Sunny, and don't hang up. All this show biz stuff has clouded your reasoning, dammit, and someone has to take the initiative. We're going to get married tonight in one of those all-night chapels, and then I'm going to hold an impromptu press conference and make an official announcement."

"You can't do this," she whispered, disbelieving. "I won't be coerced into marriage. Do you hear me?" Her fingers pressed white against the receiver.

She looked up, caught the waiting tension in Gray's body, the steely glint in his eyes, and felt a wrench of emotion. She was caught in a tug-of-war of conflicting needs and desires.

Not just her own, but Ted's and Gray's. Her stomach lurched with a premonition of disaster. He hand began to tremble.

"I'm coming up," Ted threatened. "What room are you in?"

"No," she said, her voice barely audible. "No, Ted, don't. I can't—I can't marry you."

"What? What are you saying?"

"I can't marry you," she rasped again.

There was a long stunned silence. When Ted finally spoke his voice was thin, riddled with alarm. "You mean you can't marry me *tonight* . . . don't you? Sunny?"

"I—" Her throat closed painfully.

"Sunny, my God, we grew up together. What are you saying?" Desperation edged the words. "That we're through?"

Anguish twisted through her. A wave of nostalgia built, pulling her back to the past, to the sweetness of an adolescent romance. "Oh, Ted, I don't know. I just don't know anymore. Please, I need some time to think things through, *please*."

"Time?" he questioned, his voice growing harsh. "How much time does it take? We've known each other since high school. If you don't know how you feel about me by now—" He broke off, then added bitterly. "Fine, that's just fine. Take all the time you want. I'll be in my Washington office."

The phone went dead.

A dull pain surrounded her heart. She wanted to cry. It was all swimming in her head, the past, the present, feelings intermingling until she wasn't sure what was real.

Gray took the phone from her hand gently and hung it up. She looked up slowly, met his grave expression.

"Sunny, you told him the truth. You can't marry him. You don't love him."

The confusion roiled up again, tearing at her. Ted was the man she'd cared about for most of her life. Surely she'd loved him once? What about now? Did she love Gray now?

The pain welled, constricting her heart. "I'm not sure. Oh God, I don't know—"

Gray caught her hand. "Yes, Sunny, you *do know*."

She felt the pull of his quiet certainty. How could he be so sure of her feelings when her emotions were in such turmoil? "Ted's hurt," she said, shaking her head. "He's so desperate, he wanted to marry me tonight."

"He's desperate to save his political neck."

Ironically, that made her angry. "Are you saying that he's using me, that he doesn't love me?" She fought down the urge to defend her relationship with Ted. That was crazy, wasn't it? It made no sense. Oh God, nothing made any sense. She was caught between them, trapped by loyalty to Ted, desire for Gray. Was either emotion real?

"I don't care who or what Ted loves," Gray was saying. "I want you to acknowledge what *you* feel."

His grip on her hand suddenly felt like unbearable pressure. Her head whirled with indecision. Her heart ached with each beat. The man, the entire room blurred into soft focus. She wanted, needed to be alone. Closing her eyes, she whispered, "Please go."

He let go of her hand. "Is that what you want?"

She sagged back against the headboard, suddenly exhausted. "I don't know what I want." Tears misted her eyes. *"I don't know how I feel."*

He stood up then and walked to the window, staring out. "How you feel about him...?" he asked finally. "Or me?"

His profile was pensive, expectant. A soft wave of yearning moved through her.

But Ted, there was Ted...

She felt a sharp pull at her heart and the tug-of-war began again. "Please Gray," she whispered on a shaky release of air, *"please go.* I can't think with you here. I'm so tired, and there's so much to sort out, so much...." She shut her eyes then. Just closed them for a minute. But when she opened them, he was gone.

Six

Sunny leaned back in the makeup chair and closed her eyes, trying to relax as Daphne bent over her and applied generous amounts of taupe mascara.

"Pssssst, Sunny!"

Her eyelids blinked open. Mascara sprayed like tiny black raindrops. Through the murky cloudburst, Steve peered at her from over Daphne's shoulder, his forehead ribbed with worry.

"Now you've done it," Daphne snapped, dabbing at Sunny's cheek and forehead.

"What is it, Steve?" Sunny blurted.

"Don't make me use force," he said, a grin lurking behind his furrowed expression. "I want the truth. What happened between you and Gray in Las Vegas?"

Annoyed at his dramatics, Sunny smothered the urge to boom "Nothing!" Steve had been badgering her since their return to L.A., always talking in low whispers. She suspected he had more schemes and scams going than the CIA.

All his paranoia and back-porch intrigue made her nervous.

Ted's advice came to mind. "No comment," she said, wincing as Daphne scrubbed at her cheek with a cotton ball.

"I don't get it," Steve muttered, elbowing in and batting the makeup artist's hand away. "You and Gray've been back a week, and you're about as friendly as litigants in a lawsuit. Don't tell me nothing's going on."

Daphne took a retaliatory swipe at Steve's elbow.

"We're doing our jobs aren't we?" Sunny defended. "Nobody's complaining. The show's going on."

"Yeah, sure," he said shrugging. "Only now the entertainment columns are calling it 'brownout television.' Where's the spark, Sunny? Where's the electricity? You're shorting out on me."

"You want electricity," Daphne muttered. "Hire Con Edison."

"Hey—you can be replaced," Steve warned.

"Go ahead," Daphne gritted, targeting him with the mascara wand. "Make my day."

Sunny sighed and shook her head. Steve and Daphne were two of a kind, incorrigible, and today, of all days, she couldn't deal with their carryings-on.

She ducked out of the way as Daphne brandished the wand and Steve feinted back, raising both hands in concession.

"Get out of here, you two," Sunny ordered, springing up, "Or I'll call security."

"Sit down, Star," Daphne said, turning the wand on her. "I'm not done with your face."

"And I'm not done with your attitude," Steve pitched in.

Hands on her hips, Sunny dared them to come near her.

"Okay, okay," Steve said, backing out the door. "Ruin the show, ruin my life . . . my mother's life."

"Keep smiling," Daphne advised grimly. Following Steve's lead the makeup artist left, shutting the door behind her.

Sunny sank down in the chair, her overworked nerves reveling in the silence. She laid her head back and sighed out a week's worth of pressure. Indecision had been her constant companion since the show's return from Las Vegas.

Was her engagement over?

Not if her fiancé had anything to say about it, she mused grimly. Ted had been impossible since the fiasco in Las Vegas. Ignoring her plea for "time," he'd called, written, even contacted her parents, the cheapest of shots in her opinion.

And then there was Gray. He'd kept his distance since their return. He'd respected her need for space, but his constrained behavior had telegraphed an unmistakable message: his one passionate lapse of control wouldn't be repeated.

So why did that make everything harder? *Why did that make her want him more?*

Her mind strayed back to that night in Las Vegas. Shutting her eyes, she mentally replayed the moment she'd run her fingers along his lips, how he'd taken her fingertips between his teeth.

A sinking thrill brought her upright.

"Behave yourself," she muttered, glaring at her stomach. She couldn't let one of the biggest decisions of her life be motivated by unrequited desire for Gray...or by Ted's temporary insanity for that matter. No, emotion would not short-circuit logic this time. She was in a take-charge mode. This would be a mature, thought-out decision.

She leaned back in the makeup chair, biting her lower lip as she reassessed both men, all her options. The crucial question still awaited an answer. Did she love Ted? Had she ever loved him? Yes, she realized, she had loved Ted in a sweet, simple sort of way. Hero worship, perhaps. But half a lifetime of hero worship died hard. And Ted offered her solidity, security and, in his way, devotion.

What did Gray offer?

Excitement? Discovery? Yes, life would be a perpetual discovery with a man who wanted her to rebel, to grow, to be as much woman as she could be. Her mind darted through the possibilities before coming smack up against a dead end.

Wait a minute, Sunny, she caught herself, Graham Chance has made no long-term commitments to you. He's promised you nothing. Not one word about commitment. Not one word about the future. Nothing. What is he really offering... *right now*?

Her breath caught, quivered in her throat.

A night of passion?

A warm thrill cascaded through her, stimulating her senses, tingling every pulse point to life.

Control yourself, she warned desperately. Passion or no passion, you are not a one-nighter. But the warning was no match for the powerful memories that were crowding into her mind. A giddy swirl of dark, sensual images enveloped her, penetrating her psyche... and suddenly he was entering her room again, obsession in his eyes, easing the straps of her nightgown off her shoulders, caressing her, arousing a melting ache between her thighs that soared to an urgency so sharp she nearly cried out.

On a shuddering, drawn-in breath, she sat up, wide awake now, painfully aware. She wanted that night of passion.

She wanted Gray.

Out of the chair, crossing the room, she wondered at her sanity. After a week's worth of agonized deliberation, passion had decided her future? There was something decidedly crazy about that, but she didn't dare let herself stop to think about it. Somehow, *somehow*, she knew this was the most important move she'd ever made in her life.

"Please God," she murmured, throwing open her door, rushing down the hall. "Let him be in his dressing room."

Poised to knock on his door, she froze. From a tiny corner of her fevered brain, the cool voice of reason gave it one last try. *You're letting your heart lead,* it cautioned, *basing your decision on emotion. You're going to regret—*

She rapped quickly. All her life's choices had been reasonable. This one came from the heart. This one felt right, dammit. And it was much more than passion she was choosing. It was freedom. Between Ted and her parents, she'd never made a completely independent decision in her life. Thirty years of living under someone else's thumb was enough.

She glanced at her watch, saw it was perilously close to airtime and knocked again. What would she say when he answered? Would he even care that she'd opted for freedom? Every second of delay was agony. She stared at the door so intently, she jumped when it opened.

Gray hesitated on the threshold, obviously surprised to see her. "Sunny? Something wrong?"

"No," she said, her heart beating faster. "No—I just thought maybe we could talk for a minute."

He stepped back and swung the door open.

As she walked past him, she felt a prickling race up the back of her neck. Fine hairs shivered, galvanized by an invisible charge.

He folded his arms and leaned against the doorjamb. "What's on your mind?" he asked, his voice so evenly modulated that she turned, mystified. This man was too calm to be believed.

He looked so dashing in his open-necked shirt and Italian-cut Ungaro jacket that she found herself staring. His expression was amused, patient, tinged with curiosity. Couldn't he have the decency to be at least as anxiety-stricken as she was? Yet something in the taut lift of his jaw signaled tension, *yes*—tension rigidly constrained.

He swung the door shut and glanced at his watch. "We don't have much time," he told her, one corner of his mouth easing up slightly, just enough for her to see that near-irresistible crease begin to form in his cheek.

Tense or not, he can handle himself, she thought. She exhaled a deep breath and let fly. "I've been thinking about what happened in Las Vegas."

His smile deepened, took on another meaning and melty feelings began inside her.

"I'd appreciate it if you didn't smirk while I'm trying to be serious."

He nodded, sobering.

"This has been one of the most difficult weeks of my life," she said sincerely. "I've been wrestling with some very tough questions, but I've come to a decision, and I think— I hope—it's the right one."

His eyes glinted with questions and her heart began to race.

"Good news or bad news?" he asked.

"Show time!" someone called from outside the door.

She started again. "I've decided that—"

Gray straightened expectantly.

"Let's go!" the voice yelled.

"—that Ted and I—" Oh God, *this wasn't working*. How could she bare her soul with only seconds to airtime.

"What . . . ?" Gray asked. "Ted and you *what*?"

The door creaked open and Steve's head poked in.

With a muffled moan, Sunny threw her head back and stared up at the ceiling.

Steve shot them both a pained directorial smile. "The first lesson of success, guys," he counseled. "Don't keep your fans waiting." He jerked his head in a "let's go" gesture.

A lump formed in her throat. She glanced at her watch, at Steve. She'd missed her chance. Fate . . . ? Divine intervention? Was someone trying to tell her she'd made the wrong decision?

Saved in the nick of time, the voice in her mind admonished. Stop leading with your heart!

Her courage wavering, she looked up and saw the intensity in Gray's eyes. Her throat paper dry, she mumbled, "Can't keep the fans waiting," and then she brushed past Steve and out the door.

"Hey!" Steve's voice followed her. "Did you hear that? She actually listened to me."

Time seemed to stall as Sunny negotiated her way through the show's first two segments. On the surface, her smile still worked, but inside she felt all the controlled tension of a circus high-wire act.

And her usually personable co-host had jumped the track completely. Next to her on the couch, Gray exuded a waiting menace. Between the two of them, the atmosphere on the set crackled like a slow-burning fuse.

"Stay tuned for our next guest," Gray informed the approaching camera. "We've got a multi-talented clairvoyant for you. A woman who looks at the future from every possible angle."

Watching him, Sunny felt a building urgency.

Saved in the nick of time, the voice reiterated.

An impetus moved through her. Her lips parted; her jaw twitched.

The floor manager signaled the break before the last segment. The red light blinked off.

She had to do something. She felt ready to burst!

Without a word, Gray stood up and started off the set.

Sunny sprang to her feet. "I've made my decision," she called after him. *"Ted and I are through."*

He whirled around, hesitated a split second, then rushed her, caught her by the arms. "Are you sure?" She felt his body heat, felt his intensity burning close to the surface.

In that instant she knew. "Yes . . . yes, very sure."

Something happened inside her as she looked into his eyes, something so wonderful she felt her heart go light and wobbly. A deep glow swept through her, warming every inch of her body, touching her lips with a radiant smile.

After a hesitant, heart-clutching second, Gray spoke. "I thought you'd decided to marry him." His relief came out in a rushing, husky exhalation. A vein pulsed in his temple.

"No, I've changed too much. He's changed—"

"Have you told him?"

She started to shake her head, hesitated, glancing around at the floor manager, the production staff, the entire crew. All activity ceased as they watched.

"Well—have you told him?" they asked in unison.

A nervous titter erupted. Laughter broke loose in a resounding release of tension.

Trying not to smile, Sunny warned, "Not one word goes beyond this room." Their quick nods reassured her.

"Knock it off, party animals," Steve's voice cut through from the booth. "We've got a show to put on. Hit it!"

Sunny collected herself in a frantic rush as the cameras whirred to life. "Welcome back," she said, her smile defying gravity. "And believe me when I tell you we've saved something really special for last. Our next guest is a—" not trusting herself to get it right, she glanced down at her notes "—clairvoyant, numerologist and phrenologist all rolled into one."

She stood up and extended her hand, Gray rising with her. "Meet Cosmos, the woman who can read the secrets hidden among the bumps on your head!"

A thin, timid-looking woman hovered at the edge of the set. "And here she is now—Cosmos," Sunny repeated, nodding encouragingly.

Only seconds into the segment, Sunny realized that Cosmos had a major case of stage fright. The interview wavered and lurched as both Sunny and Gray coaxed information from their guest.

First Class Romance

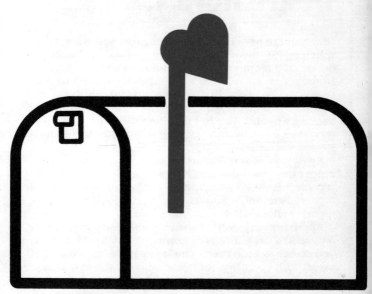

Delivered to your door by
Silhouette Desire®

Find romance at your door with 4 FREE Silhouette Desire novels!

Now you can have the intense romances you crave without searching for them. You can receive Silhouette Desire novels each month to read in your own home. Silhouette Desire novels are modern love stories for readers who want to experience firsthand *all* the joyous and thrilling emotions of women who fall in love with a passion that knows no bound. You can share in the passion and joy of their love, every month, when you subscribe to Silhouette Desire.

By filling out and mailing the attached postage-paid order card, you'll receive FREE 4 new Silhouette Desire romances (a $9.00 value) plus a FREE Folding Umbrella and Mystery Gift. You'll also receive an extra bonus: our monthly Silhouette Books Newsletter.

Approximately every 4 weeks, we'll send you 6 more Silhouette Desire novels to examine FREE for 15 days. If you decide to keep them, you'll pay just $11.70 (a $13.50 value) with no charge for home delivery and at no risk! You'll also have the option of cancelling at any time. Just drop us a note. Your first 4 books, Folding Umbrella and Mystery Gift are yours to keep in any case.

Silhouette Desire ®

A FREE Folding Umbrella and Mystery Gift await you, too!

Mail this card today for
4 FREE BOOKS
(a $9.00 value)
and a Folding Umbrella and
Mystery Gift FREE!

CLIP AND MAIL THIS POSTPAID CARD TODAY!

Silhouette ❤ _Desire_®

Silhouette Books, 120 Brighton Rd., P.O. Box 5084, Clifton, NJ 07015-9956

☐ YES! Please send me my four SILHOUETTE DESIRE novels FREE, along with my FREE Folding Umbrella and Mystery Gift, as explained in this insert. I understand that I am under no obligation to purchase any books.

NAME _____

(please print)

ADDRESS _____

CITY _____ STATE _____ ZIP _____

Terms and prices subject to change.
Your enrollment is subject to acceptance by Silhouette Books.

SILHOUETTE DESIRE is a registered trademark.

CMD4D6

Finally, in desperation, Gray suggested that Cosmos do a sample reading. "Give us a glimpse of Sunny's future," he said, deviltry lurking behind his smile, "specifically her love life."

The clairvoyant went pale. "R-read?" Her eyes fluttered shut; her body drooped.

For a horrible moment, Sunny thought the woman had passed out. But then Cosmos pressed two trembling fingers to her forehead. Her eyelids vibrated. "Your love life is in transition," she whispered, "as is the rest of your life. You are about to change course and set sail in a new direction."

"Me?" Sunny beamed and exchanged a sidelong glance with Gray. Their brief eye contact was charged with an intimacy that left her giddy. So giddy, it was a moment before she realized that Cosmos's head had slumped over. "Oh!" Sunny exclaimed, gently shaking the woman's arm.

"Cosmos," Gray said, rescuing the moment. "Got anything on me in there? How about some tips on my future?"

The clairvoyant's eyes blinked open. She focused intently on Gray, her gaze straying to his golden-brown hair. "You have a fascinating head," she said. "I'd like to read your bumps."

Wouldn't we all, Sunny thought, grinning.

Gray shrugged, obviously a little uneasy.

Cosmos walked around the couch and positioned herself behind Gray. Considerably more confident now, she shut her eyes and eased her hands into his hair. "Ummm," she murmured.

Gray's eyebrows slanted ambivalently as the clairvoyant's fingers crawled through his hair, turning his Ivy League cut into a tousled mop of gold.

"Marvelous contours," Cosmos said, her voice husky. "I feel such drive, such confidence. And here—" she made one-fingered circles on the crown of his head "—here I feel enormous strength. Ummm, yes, this elongated bump tells me he has a vigorous—" She broke off, blushing.

"Libido?" Sunny hazarded. From the corner of her eye, she saw the floor manager give her the wrap-up signal.

Oblivious, Cosmos continued circling. Her eyelids quivered shut and a look of ecstasy glowed through her thin features.

The effect my co-host has on womankind is amazing, Sunny thought, smiling inside. "I think Cosmos has discovered a new erogenous zone," she said for the camera's benefit.

She winked at Gray, an irrepressible grin breaking as she turned to the cameras. "Can the man help it if he's got irresistible bumps?"

The next week passed in a serendipitous haze as all of Sunny's fears and expectations resolved themselves, one by one, with unexpected ease.

Ted, bless his heart, did not threaten to blow up the nation's capital when she gently broke her news. He took it like a politician. He admitted that he'd seen it coming and wished her luck. His one request, which she instantly granted, was that she not break the news publicly until "a decent interval" had passed. He wanted a couple of weeks to pass the word to his associates before the news hit the media.

Even her parents had come through like troopers.

"Darling, whatever makes you happy," her mother had said, then whispered, "Is it that Chance man?"

Sunny had hung up the phone, laughed and fallen into a chair. Why hadn't somebody told her it would be this easy to change the course of her life? She'd have done it sooner!

At work, the set hummed with collective goodwill and the shared anticipation of something wonderful about to break.

After every show, Sunny rushed to Gray's dressing room for a few minutes alone with him. Stolen moments, golden moments, each brief interlude charged with desire, yet gentled by restraint and a sense of sweet promise. Every day their secret relationship grew brighter, sharper...and the edges of Sunny's world blurred into softer focus.

"Taking a *chance* on love..." Sunny sang, rushing into her dressing room in anticipation of her meeting with Gray. The morning's show, as always, had been unpredictable, in fact, it had been a near free-for-all. The Boy George Fashion Show and the herbal aphrodesiacs segment had been fun, yes, but she was anxious to escape the chaos, to be alone with Gray.

"Here I go again..." she warbled, hurrying out of her linen dress and into a vanilla cotton jump suit.

Gray's door was shut, so she tapped lightly before opening it. Disappointment flickered as she saw the empty room. Was he still on the set? she questioned, deciding to wait.

Shutting the door behind her, she let her eyes sweep over the small area, wondering if it would reveal anything of its occupant. Since admitting her feelings about Gray, she'd burned with curiosity, aware of how little she really knew about him.

She'd plied him with questions, learned that he had a younger brother, Mark, a hopeful on the pro tennis circuit—but very little else. Thinking to put Gray at ease, she'd told him about her own past at length, even shared one of her secret vices—eating Snickers bars, peanuts first, in inconsolable moments.

But no luck. Maybe she'd pressed too hard. Men are naturally more reticent, she reminded herself. Nevertheless, she was dying to know. Everything.

The state of his dressing room reclaimed her attention. He's reasonably neat, she decided, noting the suit jacket carefully arranged over the back of a chair and the men's cologne and after-shave lined up on the makeup table. A script for tomorrow's show waited on the coffee table. Peeking out from beneath it, she spotted a scribbled note.

Curiosity stoked the fire inside her.

She squinted at it from across the room. It looked like...a phone message. None of her business, of course, but since she was going to the couch anyway maybe she'd just glance—

She heard the door open and froze, midstride.

Footsteps approached from behind. Low growling sounds made her smile as strong hands eased around her waist and pulled her back against a solidly masculine form. His breath feathered through the curls at her temple. "Guess who."

"That's a tough one," she said, laughing. "What do I win if I'm right?"

"My heart, my soul, *my body*. Take your pick."

"I want them all," she breathed, twisting around to face him. "I must have them all."

His eyes sparkled with provocative lights. His hands slid to her hipbones and tugged her lower torso up against his. "Greedy woman. For that you get everything *but* my body."

Hard thighs and hipbones pressed into her softness. Vividly aware of each pressure point, she felt something else. Something stubbornly, unquestionably male. It nudged intimately against her, eliciting familiar thrills. She drew a breath, then shrugged, feigning indifference. "Two out of three isn't bad."

A chuckle erupted, husky, rich with feeling. "I can see you're devastated, so I'll give you a reprieve." Suddenly, his eyes were blindingly blue. "You can have my body—provided you take it *now*."

Brushing a kiss across her lips, he hooked an arm under her knees, picked her up and carried her to the couch.

"Gray, I—"

"No point denying you're crazy for me," he said, his voice rustling as he eased alongside her on the narrow cushions. "Your body's talking for you." He pressed two fingers to her throat, slid them down to the tapering fullness above her left breast. "Your heartbeat's off the charts, kiddo."

"Ummm," she murmured as casually as her constricted breathing would allow, "betrayed by the clinical signs of arousal again?"

"A textbook case," he said, his eyes sparkling.

She knew exactly what prize he had in store for her as his fingers combed into her hair and grabbed soft handfuls. His lips burned an ardent I-can't-wait-any-longer message into hers. Questing male heat pressed aggressively against her thigh. Lord, could she hold out this time?

Heartbeat tapped out a fast answer. Definitely *not*. One more bout with the liquid ache his closeness triggered and she'd be *his* in every possible sense of the word.

"Gray," she whispered, making no attempt to hide the desperation in her voice. "Gray, don't start what we can't finish. You know I promised myself I'd wait—at least until I can announce that Ted and I are officially over."

It wasn't quite true. Sunny knew she was using a formality to delay the inevitable, but Gray's sexual immediacy so overwhelmed her senses when they were together this way that she was filled with a crazy paralyzing fear of crossing that last barrier to intimacy.

"We'll stop," he promised, his voice husky, his hand finding her breast.

Shivering, she felt the near-telepathic energy in his fingers, felt it flood through her until every nerve ending was vibrantly alive. When the current touched her feminine parts, she gasped, "Gray—we have to stop—*now*."

With a low animal growl, he nuzzled into the curve of her neck. "You sure?"

"Yes," she breathed, pressing her hands against his chest. "This last-minute denial stuff is painful, dangerous. I'm close to taking a flyer."

He shifted back, his eyes smoky, a smile curling. "Sunny Tyler? About to do something impetuous?"

Laughter gurgled up. "*About* to do something impetuous? I haven't done anything else since I met you."

He laughed with her. And then his smile faded as he looked down at her. With the abruptness of a flash of lightning, desire reignited his gaze. "You're quite a woman, Sunny. Exciting, unpredictable."

The sharp stir of pleasure she felt told her to move, and move quickly. She maneuvered out from under him, shifted to the edge of the couch and sat there, forcing the shakiness from her body, the emotion from her voice. "Unpredictable, maybe, frustrated, definitely."

He pulled himself up, heaved out a breath and held his head in his hands. "I'll second that 'definitely.'"

As she sat there, recovering, a white fleck on the floor caught her attention. Her eyes focused on the note she'd spotted earlier.

She stole a glance at Gray, his head still bowed.

Her eyes returned to the note. It lay there, abandoned. If she didn't pick it up, it might get lost, right? Leave it alone, she told herself. Curiosity has been known to kill inquisitive cats. But the attraction was too strong. She bent and retrieved it.

Gray's head lifted abruptly.

Startled, Sunny glanced at the paper in her hand, her eyes flitting across the message.

Gray. Please call me. I want to make up for all the mistakes I've made.

                                          Kristin

"Don't," he warned. His hand reached over and took the note from her.

For a minute, she couldn't move, couldn't speak. "Who is Kristin?" she asked finally, each word a forced whisper.

"No one." His voice came from miles away. "She has nothing to do with you and me."

Still, she couldn't look at him. "Who is she?" she rasped again, hanging on to the arm of the couch.

"Sunny," he said, moving closer. "You saw a message that wasn't intended for you. Forget it, dammit. It has nothing to do with us."

Gray slid next to her, but Sunny shook her head and motioned him away. Muttering an expletive, he rose, walked to the makeup table and sat on the edge, facing her.

The air seemed to thicken with suffocating silence.

As she brushed jerkily at the crumpled collar of her jump suit, preparing to leave, determined to leave, the dressing room door creaked open.

Steve's animated features grinned at her, a jarring counterpoint to the tension.

"Brush off your tuxedos, stars, we're gonna party," he sang, tapping a drum beat on the door before swinging it open. His myopic eyes did a quick but thorough search, looking from Gray at the table to Sunny on the far end of the couch. "Cheer up, kids, the word is party!"

"We're not in the mood at the moment," Gray muttered, a low threat in his voice.

"Not now," Steve persisted, striding into the room, "Saturday. Saturday night! Hey—I'm talking about the biggest bash Hollywood's seen since the infamous studio orgies."

"Wine and cheese at your apartment?" Gray inquired sarcastically.

"No, wise guy. Beluga caviar and Dom Perignon at Bill Blanchard's Holmby Hills estate."

Gray's brows lifted. Sunny perked up a little. She looked at Steve.

"All right," he said, arms thrown out. "This is more like it. The fun starts at six. At five-thirty, you will each be picked up by limo."

Sunny's heart thumped to life. "What's going on?"

Steve grinned and winked. "Come to the party and find out."

Gray flicked the tumbled hair from his forehead. "Why would Blanchard be inviting us to a party?"

"Steve," Sunny implored, "tell us what's going on."

The producer shook his head, his face still wreathed in a maddening smile.

"Listen, Freedkin," Gray warned. "We don't need any more surprises right now, so quit playing games."

Steve raised his hands. "All right, all right, I'll tell you this much. Blanchard's juggling the network's daytime schedule. He's making changes, big changes. Be ready to knock 'em dead, kids, cause this party's the biggest callback of your life."

"He's decided? We're going network?" Sunny asked.

"Deciding," Steve corrected, holding up two pinched fingers together. "But it's this close."

Gray walked over to Steve and grabbed his hand. The two of them laughed and engaged in a vigorous arm-slapping handshake.

Their elation filled Sunny with wonder. That close? To success?

"Come here, Sunshine," Steve said laughing, waving her over.

She stood up shakily, happy and sad all at once. She ran to Steve, threw her arms around him.

"Hey, baby," he said, rocking her back and forth. "I think we're about to grab on to a dream, Sunny. And we're going to ride this one all the way."

Tears filled her eyes as he whirled her around. After he set her on her feet, he stepped back and peered at her. "Aww, look," he said softly, his smile going crooked. "You gonna cry? Happy?"

"Yes," she said, nodding. "I am. I'm happy."

Through a smiling veil of tears she saw Gray watching her. Sadness mingled with her joy. She wanted to laugh, she wanted desperately to cry. A silent question filled her mind. *Who is she,* Gray?

Seven

The jeweled towers of Century City shimmered past the darkened windows of the white stretch limo as it purred along the 405 Freeway toward Holmby Hills. Releasing a tense sigh, Sunny glanced over at her escort.

Steve rolled his eyes heavenward. "Are you listening up there? I swear I'll donate half my salary to charity if you'll work with me tonight. Let's bring this party off without a hitch, okay? Whadaya say? Deal?"

"Steve, stop praying," Sunny pleaded. "You're making me nervous."

He nodded, withdrawing into rigid preoccupation.

Settling back, she rearranged the black satin and lace skirt of her gown. She couldn't deny that she felt glamorous tonight. Satin rustled softly with her movements. And the feel of black lace—all the way down to her peekaboo teddy with ribboned garters—stirred a sense of daring within her.

Tonight's gala at Bill Blanchard's Gothic-Romanesque castle hidden high in the hills promised to be the industry's social event of the season. "The party that has all of tinsel town talking," promised entertainment and gossip columnists who'd picked up rumors of an impending announcement.

Reporters had been waiting outside Sunny's condo since dusk, ready with flashbulbs and questions when Steve had arrived in the limo to pick her up. But this time they were far more interested in her career plans than her alleged romantic escapades; she'd even heard traces of respect in their voices as they inquired about her television future.

Sunny shut her eyes, anticipation rippling through her like a current. Only one thing could subdue her sheer excitement tonight. *Only one man.*

Heaving a deep sigh, she felt Steve's eyes on her.

"Seen this yet?" he asked, pulling a tabloid from his tuxedo jacket and holding it up for her to read.

The headlines shouted: Sunny Dumps Congressman. Is She Still Feuding With Her Co-Host Lover?

She winced at the crass insensitivity of the headlines, the outright lies the story contained. "Several days ago," she said, nodding. "It's old news." She'd made the mistake of reading that particular article and afterward, near tears, had called Ted to explain that someone on the set must have leaked the information. He'd talked her out of suing the publishers for every penny they had.

Steve tossed the paper aside. "Forget it, you're a free woman now." Seconds stretched as he studied her. "So... what does all this mean for you and Gray?"

She looked away. "There's a problem," she said finally, posing the question that had been on her lips for days. "How much do you know about Gray's past?"

The producer's eyes narrowed paranoically. "Why? Has he done something wrong? A criminal record?" He grabbed her arm. "What is it, Sunny? Drugs—?"

"Of course not," she assured him, realizing she'd hit his panic button.

"Damn," he breathed. "You scared ten years off me. I've had nightmares about something going wrong tonight. What do you mean—Gray's past?"

There was no discreet way to phrase it. "I have reason to think he may be involved with another woman."

"Whaaat?"

She hesitated, wondering whether to go on. Her mouth felt as dry as dust. "Have you ever heard of a woman named Kristin?"

His forehead creased. "Don't think so. Who is she?"

"Nobody, I hope," she said, exhaling. "Forget I even mentioned her, okay?" Looking out the window, she realized they'd left the freeway and turned onto the twisting road that would take them up into the hills.

"Another woman?" Steve was muttering. "Impossible."

When she turned back, he took both her hands. "You've got nothing to worry about, Sunshine. Gray's nuts about you. He hasn't looked at another woman since the day he met you."

"Really?" She smiled through a cloud of skepticism.

"I swear it, Sunny. I know when a man's in love, and you've got that guy's heart tied up in granny knots."

Steve's manner was entirely too glib to suit her, but it didn't stop her from wanting to believe what he'd said. She decided to settle for the line about Gray's not looking at other women. And that was only because she hadn't caught Gray at it, unless you counted Helga.

Steve gave her hands a little shake. "The guy's wild about you. Take my advice—if you want a relationship with him, stop turning him on and off like a faucet."

She smiled despite herself. "Subtle you're not."

"Subtle, hell. I'm right."

The limo veered left and pulled to a stop at a gated entrance manned by an army of security guards. Sunny noticed reporters and a flux of curious onlookers lining the road.

Excitement built within her again, coupled with a pervasive feeling that none of this was really happening. That it had to be a dream.

The gates eased open and they drove through into an emerald landscape swept with formal gardens, marble fountains and reflecting pools. Sunny hardly knew where to look.

She'd heard Bill Blanchard was a multimillionaire in his own right, a man whose sole motivation was the industry's challenge, its killing pace. Still, nothing had prepared her for this grandeur.

As they continued along the winding road, the sculptured landscape gave way to a dark, twelfth-century Gothic forest. Her eyes had barely adjusted to the murky light before a full-blown Romanesque fortress, complete with flying buttresses and celestory windows, appeared in a blaze of floodlights.

"Damn," Steve said under his breath as they pulled up to a soaring rib-vaulted archway. Guards in metal breastplates and chain mail lined the entrance.

"It looks like a ride at Disneyland," Sunny ventured, feeling faint-hearted.

Steve's voice was hushed, reverent. "Blanchard's the new creative force behind RBC programming. Word's out he's an eccentric genius. I think I believe it." He turned to Sunny, an exultant grin breaking. "This is going to be the night of our lives," he whispered. "Everybody who counts is inside that crazy castle, kid. Let's go."

A guard clanked over to help Sunny from the limo and escort her down the arcade. She felt like a medieval princess as massive doors opened onto a cathedrallike entry.

A long hallway led to pillared arches that preceded a torch-lit ballroom of dizzying dimensions. Hesitating, she felt Steve's hand at her elbow. "Come on," he coaxed. "Let's storm the citadel."

"Wait," she whispered, awed by the flaming torches and standing cast-iron candelabra. "Let me get my bearings first." Jugglers, tumblers and wandering musicians entertained along the room's periphery.

Among the glamorous revelers, Sunny spotted several people she'd interviewed on the show. *The rich and famous set.* They'd been in her domain then. Now she was entering theirs'. Goosebumps traveled up her arms.

A waiter in monk's robes appeared with a tray. "Champagne?"

Steve took two glasses, handing one to her.

Sipping exquisitely dry Dom Perignon, she stared, wide-eyed at the spectacle before her. Blanchard hadn't limited his guest list to television celebrities, she quickly realized, spotting a playboy race-car driver and a Nobel Prize-winning author.

Everywhere she looked, hooded waiters hovered with trays of toast points, jet-black caviar and canapés that resembled works of art. Sunny nearly dropped her champagne when she noticed the silver-headed star of a prime-time soap smiling at her from across the room.

Was there something wrong with her dress? No, by gosh, that was a smile of admiration. She smiled back.

Steve's eyes darted about the room. "I'll find our host. You find Gray," he ordered, "and when you do, kiss and make up."

Had he read her thoughts? All her concerns about another woman seemed irrelevant in this wondrous time warp. She breathed in deeply, absorbing the room's magic. The evening stretched before her, beckoning, full of promise.

After all, she reasoned, Kristin could be anybody, a relative, perhaps. The fact that Gray hadn't wanted to talk about her only meant that he considered it a personal matter, not that he was necessarily hiding something.

"Go ahead, find Blanchard," she told Steve, nodding as a soap opera actress she'd interviewed walked by, "I'll be fine."

Making her way through the crowds, Sunny greeted people as she searched. So what if Gray has another woman, she decided recklessly, I'll fight her for him. *After all, a woman who wears a peekaboo teddy and ribboned garters gets what she wants.*

She lost a breath as Gray moved into her line of vision. Her immediate impression was of a still profile in crowning blond and sunbronzed hues. Looking nothing less than magnificent in his midnight-black tuxedo, he conversed with another guest.

She moved toward him spontaneously, slowing, halting as she recognized the object of his serious blue gaze. Madeline Downs. The flame-haired film star he'd interviewed several times. Their rapt conversation excluded everyone in the room.

Including Sunny.

Responding as though Gray had said something wonderful, Madeline laughed, a low vibrant sound, rich with insinuation. The actress rose on tiptoes and feathered a kiss across Gray's cheek, her lips brushing the corner of his mouth.

Sunny faltered, stepped back. Jealousy stung like the flick of a whip, irrational, heart piercing, its intensity beyond her experience. *Look away,* she told herself. *Pretend you haven't seen him.*

A hand touched her shoulder. Whipping around, she stood face-to-face with a tall, almost gaunt man. A mustache and a thatch of wild black hair added to his eccentric mien. RBC's programming chief? She felt the color drain from her face. "Mr. Blanchard?" Her voice quavered, taut as a violin string.

Steve hovered at Blanchard's side, watchful, as nervous as an expectant father. "I decided it was time you two met," Steve said, his voice full of forced jocularity.

"Long overdue," Blanchard agreed, nodding gallantly. "So—I finally get to meet Barbie incarnate. You've become quite a phenomenon, Miss Tyler—may I call you, Sunny? No doubt you've heard it a million times, but you are breathtaking in person."

Warmth seeped back into her cheeks as she took his outstretched hand. "No one's ever said it quite that way," she said on a rushed exhalation.

"Steve tells me my little announcement tonight will be a surprise to you."

So there *would* be an announcement. He'd made a decision. "Yes, Steve's a master of suspense—" She searched her producer's face for clues. "He keeps us on our toes."

"Let me assure you," Blanchard said, smiling mysteriously, "there will be surprises—for both of you."

He winked at Sunny and her heart jumped rhythm.

Steve's worried expression smoothed into a smile as Blanchard turned to him and said, "I believe I'd like some time alone with this lovely woman."

"I'm history," Steve said, grasping the situation immediately. He backed away, nodding. "Enjoy."

"Charming in his way," Blanchard said indulgently. "But much too nervous. Always talking shop."

"He can't help himself," Sunny explained. "The show is like oxygen to him."

"And to you?" Blanchard's dark, insomniac eyes studied her.

"It's important to me, too," she said, glancing over her shoulder just in time to see Gray and the redhead laugh and touch champagne glasses. Jealousy ripened to anger. "Possibly the most important thing in my life."

"Good, good." Blanchard's nod of approval prompted a waitress to rush over offering quail eggs and beluga *ma-*

lossol. Sunny had a dangerous thought. How would Madeline look wearing toast points and caviar?

Another glance told Sunny that Gray had seen her. She felt a quiver of satisfaction as his tight blue gaze fastened on her and Bill Blanchard. Two can play this game, she thought, surprisingly bold. Maybe knowing another man found her attractive was just the nudge Gray needed.

She smiled expansively at Blanchard, feeling a little thrill as she peeked and saw Gray's narrowing eyes. This was fun. She felt brazen, almost daring. She'd never attempted to arouse a man's jealous nature before. Her relationship with Ted hadn't inspired such intrigues.

"I'm one of your biggest fans," Blanchard was telling her. "You have a gift for turning potential disaster into high comedy that could never be scripted."

"Thank you," she murmured, immensely pleased. "On live television, we call it survival."

"Exactly." Blanchard laughed and lifted two champagne flutes off a passing tray.

Sunny accepted hers demurely. "Couldn't you just give me a hint, Mr. Blanchard?" she asked with a smile. "About your surprise, I mean?"

His eyes glinted with undisguised interest. "I insist that you call me Willy. All my intimate friends do. And now—" He held out his glass. "Instead of a hint, a toast. To you, Miss Tyler, Sunny, the rising star who may soon have this industry in orbit around her."

Blushing wildly, she held her glass up to his. From the corner of her eye, she saw Gray, alone now, his legs braced wide, his arms folded. His eyes held a blue force that hit her like a physical blow. She took a generous swallow of champagne.

Gray signaled one of the waiters. "Think you could find me a double Scotch somewhere?"

"Sure, back in a minute." The monk in the floor-length robe hustled away.

Undoing the crimson bow tie on his tuxedo with a quick jerk of his fingers, Gray continued to observe Sunny's antics with Bill Blanchard.

She knows exactly what she's doing, he decided. She's trying to get me going. *And it's working.* She knows that, too. A narrow smile formed. If she isn't careful, I may throw her over my shoulder and carry her off...

He felt a tightening in his loins as an erotic scenario played through his mind. Cool it, he told himself automatically. The woman is a free agent. She has a right to talk to anyone she chooses.

The words should have worked, but they didn't. When Blanchard slid a hand around Sunny's waist to point out a juggler's performance, Gray's hands curled into fists.

He took a deep breath, forcing himself to ease up. She'd aroused a flare of possessiveness in him, and watching her with Blanchard stoked the fire. But he couldn't help it...she fascinated him. The excited sparkle in her eyes, the new bravado in her style.

She's changing, he thought, blossoming like an exotic flower. She was becoming her own woman, and watching it happen took his breath away.

The mumbled word "Scotch?" distracted him.

"Thanks." He nodded and took the glass absently. The liquor burned his throat, eased his tension. He took another swallow and told himself to go find Madeline, but his eyes returned to Sunny.

All along, he'd fought to keep his possessiveness in check with her. The last thing she needed was another Ted. A butterfly just out of its cocoon needed to fly—and she was exactly that. Fragile, beautiful, finding her wings. Fragments of an old proverb came to him. Something about a butterfly lighting on an open hand...

A punch on the arm brought him back to the present. "Hey, man, you're staring," Steve said, looking over at Sunny and Blanchard. "That's not polite."

Gray silenced him with a look.

"Just a joke, man," the producer assured him, stepping out of the way as musicians plucking ancient wooden instruments pranced by.

Easing back by Gray's side, Steve's voice dropped low. "Sunny suspects you've got another woman. I tried to talk her out of it—"

Musical sounds floated their way as Sunny laughed at something Blanchard was telling her. She placed a hand on her hip and pointed a playful finger at the programming chief.

Gray's eyes jerked to her body, soft, slender, sheathed in lace. Small, golden breasts swelled over the black satin bodice.

Gray went rigid as the RBC executive traced a finger along her shoulder and down her arm.

"Relax man," Steve said, catching his arm. "It's PR that's all. He likes her. He likes the show."

"I don't like him," Gray cut in. "If he touches her like that again—"

"Are you crazy?" Steve hissed. "That's Bill Blanchard. He can touch any shoulder he wants!"

"Any shoulder but that one," Gray said, jerking his arm free.

Steve darted in front of him, blocking his path. *"Wait a minute,"* he pleaded. "What are you going to do?"

"Relax, I'm not going to break up the party. I just want to talk to Sunny."

"No! *Not now.*" Steve feinted right and left, anticipating Gray's advances. "Okay, listen," he said desperately. "I've got an idea. I'll distract Blanchard for a while. That'll give you a chance to take her aside—"

"Distract him how?"

"Let me take care of that."

Gray glanced over and saw Sunny brushing something from the programming chief's lapel. She peeked around Blanchard's shoulder, met Gray's fixed stare and cocked her head rebelliously. Eyes bright, she thrust out her delicate chin, stubborn as all hell.

An impulse jolted through Gray. "Distract him," he told Steve, his eyes never leaving Sunny's. Okay Sunny, he telegraphed mentally. If you're looking for some excitement, you've got it!

The unspoken message traveled between them like a raw snap of energy.

From her position of power near Blanchard, Sunny shifted, suddenly nervous. She watched Gray cautiously, trying to read his mood. He looked angry, yet at the same time a narrow smile had formed on his lips. Meanwhile, Steve was rounding up tumblers and jugglers. *What was going on?*

As Gray and Steve started toward her, she took hold of Blanchard's arm. "Willy—why don't we get some fresh air?" she suggested, coaxing him around and toward an arched opening that led to a flagstone terrace.

Gray overtook them. "In a hurry?" he asked.

"Well, if it isn't Chance," Blanchard said equably.

"You've met?" Sunny wondered aloud.

Blanchard threw an arm around Sunny and pulled her close. "This woman is something special, isn't she, Chance?"

Steve shouldered in. "Will you look at that?" he said, directing their attention to a group of approaching tumblers. "Aren't they terrific?"

Onlookers murmured their approval as the acrobats somersaulted, flipped and cartwheeled their way toward Blanchard and his small party in the center of the room.

In a dazzling display of precision they ended up in a single line and took a bow. The crowd applauded.

Watching the performance, Sunny sensed a presence behind her. A hand curled around her wrist. "I want to talk to you," Gray said. The words vibrated intimately near her ear.

"Not now," she whispered back, not about to be intimidated.

"Yes, *now*," he pressed. "It's important."

"Tell it to Madeline." Slicing him a "take that" glare, she peeled his hand off her wrist.

His eyes flashed like light ricocheting off glass. "Are you coming with me or do I have to—"

The crowd burst with more applause.

"Come on," he grated, reaching for her.

She jerked away. "Touch me and you'll never use that hand again."

A gasp from behind drew her attention. The acrobats had formed a human pyramid. The top man wobbled, sending a ripple effect through his support system. Undaunted, he crouched, placed his hands on the lower man's shoulders and executed a painfully slow and unsteady headstand.

"Bravo!" Steve yelled. The crowd clapped enthusiastically.

Gray eased the hair back from Sunny's ear. His hip nudged hers. "I warn you," he whispered, "if you're going to get physical, I'll win. I'm bigger than you are."

"So I've noticed." She glanced up and the sheer wickedness in his eyes stirred her. *Darn, that melty feeling was starting again.* "Go ahead, try something," she bluffed, refusing to succumb to his magnetic half-smile. "I know a feminist lawyer."

Another gasp pulled her attention back to the entertainment. Her eyes widened. The pyramid swayed in a wide arc as the top man fought to return to his upright position.

"Better get out of the way," Gray cautioned, seizing her by the waist, pulling her back up against him. "Come with me," he breathed in her ear, "I want—I *need* to talk to you."

Her heart gave an odd jerk as his arms tightened around her waist. "All right," she agreed, looking at her watch. "Just five minutes; any more than that and Willy will miss me."

"Willy?" he growled.

She twisted from his arms, grinning, and he grabbed her hand. "The patio," he said, bringing her with him.

They didn't make it two steps.

The crowd's exclamations snapped them around just in time to see the pyramid dip wildly, forcing its bottom rung into some furious footwork.

"No!" Steve croaked. "Don't fall! I didn't pay you guys to fall!" Arms stretched wide, he ran to the human wall and tried to buttress it. "Look out!" he screamed at RBC's chief.

Blanchard leaped out of range.

"Damn." Gray laughed, a throaty groan. "Steve's in deep trouble. I'd better help."

"Don't you dare!" Sunny latched on to his arm.

The pyramid swayed back, rocked east, west, then rebounded forward. With a mighty grunt, Steve braced himself against the inexorable forces of inertia and gravity—and lost. The wall lurched, buckled, and came tumbling down, taking *L.A. Heartbeat*'s producer out with it.

Unfettered by Steve's reach, the top man leaped free, hit the ground and grabbed for the first thing in his path.

It happened to be Bill Blanchard.

A collective "Oh no!" erupted.

"No!" Sunny screamed, hanging on to Gray. They watched helplessly as the entangled television exec and tumbler careened toward oblivion.

The stunned crowd parted like the Red Sea as a blur of arms and legs flashed past them in what could have been a bizarre beer-barrel-polka exhibition. The flailing dancers continued through an open archway and out onto the patio until they finally spiraled from sight.

Seconds later, a teeth-rattling crash shook the candela-bra.

A low groan dragged Sunny's attention back to the fallen pyramid. Steve pushed through the pile, his glasses hanging off one ear, a canapé plastered on his lapel. "Get me a doctor," he moaned, crawling on hands and knees toward Sunny.

She rushed to him, Gray right behind her.

"Where's Blanchard?" he mumbled.

"Don't ask," Sunny and Gray said in unison.

Steve's head snapped up; he searched their tense expressions and let out a low moan. "My mother wanted me to be a dentist. Why didn't I listen?"

"Look—he's all right!" the crowd cried as the programming chief staggered back through the archway, two monks propping him up.

"If you would all be so kind," Blanchard rasped, his wild-eyed visage directed at Steve. "I'd like to make my announcement while I still can."

Eight

I'm finished. I'll never work in television again," Steve moaned as Gray helped him to his feet.

"Shhh," Sunny cautioned, secretly afraid he might be right. Having no idea how to console him, she brushed off his tux and propped his bent glasses on his nose.

Blanchard stood in the archway, unaided now. The guests watched expectantly as he shrugged his tux jacket into place, straightened his tie and squared his shoulders.

Such resilience, Sunny marveled as someone scurried up and handed him a cordless mike.

"Let's hear it for Willy," a reveler called out. As the programming chief held up a hand to quiet the crowd, flashbulbs exploded. Sunny turned around, startled. Someone had let the press into the room?

"Our Steve Freedkin puts on quite a show, doesn't he?" Blanchard deadpanned, rubbing his neck. "I just wish he'd warned me that I was the star. I'd have hired a stuntman." An ironic smile wavered. "I'll bet you're all wondering how

I'm going to follow that act. Well, I can't think of a better way than to pass on some exciting news. At our Annual Affiliates Convention next week, I'll be announcing the new fall lineup, but RBC's not going to make you wait until next season for 'break-out television.'" He held his hands up to quell the noise and blinding pops of light. "We have a blockbuster coming up this very summer—"

"This summer?" Steve questioned hoarsely.

Sunny held her breath.

"I'm talking about *L.A. Heartbeat*, friends." More flashes flared and snapped. "We've had our eye on that show for some time now," he continued, signaling an aide, who passed him a newspaper clipping. "To quote a well-known television critic, '*L.A. Heartbeat* is about *chemistry*. It's a funny, sexy, damn wonderful show.'"

Sunny began to breath again.

Bulbs snapped and applause built as Blanchard waved Sunny, Gray and Steve up beside him. "Ladies and gentlemen, I give you *chemistry*." He swept a hand toward Gray and Sunny. "These two hot properties have generated a whole new concept, 'Electric Television.'" Without wasting a motion, Blanchard slapped Steve soundly on the back. "And this is the showman who masterminded it all."

Unaware of Steve's soft groan, Blanchard beamed back to the crowd. "RBC's led the pack for half a decade now because we give our viewers what they want. And we're about to do it again in a big way. Next month, RBC will hit the prime-time airwaves with *Esprit*, the newest concept in television magazine formats . . ."

Prime time. Sunny's fingers flew to her mouth. Gray's hand caught hers, steadying.

Blanchard continued, shouting over the crowd's shocked buzzing. "Celebrity spots, entertainment news, gossip, *controversy*—we'll have it all." He threw out an encompassing arm. "And who else to host the hottest new show in television than this high-profile, high-powered team."

Sunny faced the approaching crowd with an astonished smile. This was a dream, right? She'd wake up any minute now, right...? The steady heat of Gray's hand, of his body next to hers assured her it was real, frighteningly real.

Grinning faces swarmed around her, hands grabbed hers, mouths brushed her cheeks. "How do you feel, Sunny?" a reporter called. "Were you surprised?" another questioned. In all the congratulatory chaos, she lost touch with Gray. "Thank you. Yes—I'm thrilled—" she heard herself saying.

The sound of a gong vibrated through the room. "Dinner is served," announced a shrouded figure carrying a torch. "This way, please."

Sunny felt herself pulled along with the momentum of the crowd, saw Bill Blanchard and Steve waiting for her up ahead.

"Ever been kidnapped?" a voice from behind inquired darkly. Before she could turn, strong sure hands took possession of her shoulders, forced her out of the flow of bodies and through a narrow archway. The steady grip propelled her through a winding tunnellike passage and out into the clinging darkness and wildflower fragrances of an untended garden.

"But dinner—" she said as the hands whirled her around and pressed her up against a granite wall.

"They'll manage without us." Whispering shadows defined Gray's features with disturbing clarity. The moon lit his eyes.

The stony chill of granite assailed Sunny's bare skin. As her eyes fought to adjust to the starless night, she felt Gray as a tangible presence closing in around her. To her heightened senses, he hovered like a night devil, the silver glow of heaven silhouetting his body.

She lost the words that were forming in her mind, lost every last remnant of reason to the incandescent form that held her.

Silent, he bent over her, tipped her chin and touched her lips, burning them with fire and ice whisperings . . . hushed intelligible intimacies. His soft, searing mouth made hers want more, so much more. "I've been waiting all night to get you alone," he said finally. "Sunny, we have to talk."

The last statement brought a blink of confusion . . . and then the tiniest shiver of reality. Yes, he had something to tell her. Clearing her throat, she managed an uneven question. "It's about Kristin, isn't it?"

She felt his hands drop away. "Yes." He shifted back then, breaking their connection. "I told you Kristin had nothing to do with you and me. It was—is—the truth." From what seemed a great distance, he reached out to touch her face, a fleeting tenderness.

"You aren't involved with her?"

"I was . . . involved."

"But not now."

"That's right."

"And you can't tell me about it."

"No," he said bluntly. "I can't. It's complicated. There's someone else involved."

She hesitated, caught, her intuition working overtime. "All right," she said finally, simply.

"All right? What does that mean?"

She smiled up at him incautiously. "I've decided to believe you. I have no reason not to."

Shadows danced with his smile. "You're getting damn cocky, you know that. I like it."

"There are lots of things you're going to like about me," she said provocatively, and then, at the look on his face, immediately wished she hadn't.

"Oh, I'm sure of it." He moved to her, feathering his hands up her bare arms and bringing them to rest on her shoulders. "I can think of a couple I like already." He trailed his fingers along the arch of her neck to her earlobe and back down. "Like this outrageous throat."

She shivered as his other hand slid, palm down, to rest across the delicate ridges of her collarbone. His fingers spread lightly, then took her breath away with their firm, deep pressure against her flesh.

Questioning, she looked up and felt the pull of his eyes. A flush warmed, tingled her skin. The invading hand lightened to a caress, easing down with heart-catching deliberateness until it hovered just above the shadowy separation of her breasts.

His flesh touched down on hers with a vibrant gasp of sensation. Her breathing quickened painfully. "Gray," she whispered, moving to him.

He shook his head, his other hand combing into her hair. "Not yet, Sunny," he cautioned huskily. "Despite what you're feeling now, you're not ready yet, and even if you were, this isn't the place."

She reacted as though stung, chagrin warming her face. Her heart gave an odd jerk at the look in his eyes.

"That wasn't a rejection," he assured her. "There's an incredibly sexy woman hiding inside Sunny Tyler—" his breath caressed her lips with a warm puff of air "—and when the time is right, I'm going to be the man to introduce you to her."

Sunny threw open the lanai doors and let the heavy scent of Plumeria drug her with its sweetness. The tropical evening held just the right degree of warmth and the ocean's offshore breeze lifted her hair away from her face and ruffled it gently.

She felt gloriously alive, hardly able to believe that she was finally in Hawaii after three weeks of nonstop travel and promotion for the new show. She'd been in twelve different states, hit nearly every major talk show on the radio-and-television circuit and been subjected to interminable photo sessions and media interviews.

Esprit had become the most highly-publicized show of the summer replacement season. Sunny found it hard to keep her feet on the ground with hopes running so high and wild. Tomorrow would be their premiere broadcast.

She threw her head back and breathed in the fragrant air. *Tomorrow she would see Gray.* Anticipation rushed through her, warm, stroking, a living thing. She hugged herself tightly.

The week after Blanchard's party she and Gray had been sent off on separate publicity tours, while Steve remained in L.A. to work out any remaining technical details and polish the new show's format to a high gloss.

She'd missed Gray terribly. Being without him, except for their rushed telephone calls, had made her realize how important he'd become in her life. She longed for his handsome smiling face, the gentle sparkle in his blue eyes that signaled he was putting her on. And another quality she'd never appreciated until now—a wonderful sense of stability that struck a chord of reason and held constant through all the hype and promotional chaos.

Their brief telephone calls had become the eye of the hurricane for her, the soul of the storm. And yet, for all his strength, the vivid picture of him that clung in her mind was a darkened silhouette with moonlit eyes . . . the *night creature, mysterious, imminently dangerous*. The man who'd promised to awaken her to her own hidden sensuality.

She walked back to her opened suitcase and lifted out a wine-colored French lace teddy. As she acknowledged the silky fabric's implicit seductiveness, a fear-edged fascination arrested her. She squeezed her eyes shut. Her heart began to pound. Was she ready?

Her body responded with a creeping warmth. In her darkened mind, a soft light came on . . . and Gray was beside her, touching her, loving her, stroking her to trembling excitement. All detail converged in a sensual blur as she felt his hands caressing her, felt the weight of his body on her...

Her quiver of pleasure became a sigh filled with a plaintive, erotic sound.

She dropped the teddy abruptly. Had that primitive cry from from Sunny Tyler? Her once-timid sensuality seemed to have taken on a life of its own, ready to emerge, full-blown at the slightest provocation.

Gray is responsible for this, she decided, not sure whether she should thank him or call out the vice squad.

She smiled and pressed her fingers to her lips. *Wow,* if her imagination could whip up such wantonness, what would happen when she had Gray himself to deal with?

She felt the pull of inner conflict. She wanted to cling to the familiarity she'd felt with Ted. No surprises, no risks, no nerve-shattering discoveries. Even their essentially unfulfilling relationship seemed preferable to the startling feelings Gray aroused. At least with Ted she knew what to expect.

But with the feeling of safety a heaviness settled in on her. *She couldn't go back.* She had to move with this new compelling momentum, to go where it took her. It was time to grow up, to open up to life. A shiver of apprehension set off the automatic trillings of an alarm inside her.

She sank down on the bed, determined to ignore it. Resisting the urge to draw up into a ball, she lay very still, dozing, drifting toward sleep...until the telephone's jangle startled her awake.

"Yes," she said, hearing a mumbled reply. The voice sounded familiar but made no sense. She stared at the receiver, turned it around and said "Hello?" into the mouthpiece.

"Hello to you, too," Gray replied, laughing.

"You! Where are you?" She glanced at the clock. "You're supposed to be on a flight here at this very moment."

"I'm already here at this very moment."

"Where?"

"Here," he laughed. "The Hawaiian Reefs Hotel. I got to thinking about you, canceled my afternoon booking and took the first plane out. I'm on the seventh floor, the room directly under yours. Hear that?"

She listened hard. "Hear what?"

"I just pounded on my ceiling, which also happens to be your floor."

"I don't think so," she said, chuckling. "I'm on the sixth floor."

"You're where? You mean I just woke up some jet-lagged tourist? Get ready for some company. I'm coming down before whoever's above me decides to—"

"You're coming here?" She looked at the French lace teddy. "Tonight?"

"Is that a problem?" he asked.

If she said yes, he'd think her a coward. "No—no problem. We'll order room service. We'll talk. We'll catch up on everything you've been doing."

"I've been doing exactly what you've been doing—running for airplanes, guesting on talk shows."

"Umm, right."

"Sunny...don't you want to see me?"

"Oh, Gray, *yes*, of course, I want to see you." I'm dying to see you, she admitted silently, it's just that I'm also a little bit terrified.

"Give me five minutes," he said.

She hung up the phone and looked at the teddy again. She'd brought her chenille robe, hadn't she?

She was hurrying into a velour exercise outfit when he knocked. Urging the jacket's zipper up to her chin, she opened the door and found him propped against the frame, casually resplendent in white shorts and a loose-fitting, V-neck shirt.

His softly mussed hair and provocative near-smile set a butterfly loose in her stomach. The one gorgeous crimson orchid he held in his hand turned the butterfly into a flock.

"Can I come in?"

She nodded, took the orchid and stood back, feeling a little silly in sweats and tennis shoes, not to mention warm.

"Been jogging?"

"Not exactly." Actually, she had once, two or three years ago. As he walked past her, she gave the door a quick discreet kick.

He's really here, she thought, swallowing, unable to help but notice how his long, well-muscled symmetry filled the room. He's here and I'm a free woman. No barriers. *Nothing to stop us.* A spark of fear ignited the flutter near her eye.

He spotted it immediately. "What is it?" he asked, coming to her.

"It's nothing," she lied, aware that he was watching, waiting. "I guess I'm just feeling a little awkward. It's been so long—"

Taking her arms, he brought her closer. "You're still afraid aren't you? Of me, of what could happen between us. And maybe even . . . yourself?"

Why did he have to be so *unequivocal*? "Yes . . . to all of the above," she said finally, having some difficulty meeting his eyes. This wasn't going the way she'd fantasized. He was so real, so flesh and blood male, so *here*.

He lifted her chin and she blurted, "Oh, Gray, why me? Why not some uninhibited woman who can give herself freely? You need a wild, sultry-type female."

Laughing softly, he drew his finger down the straight line of her nose before kissing its up-tilted top. "I have a wild sultry-type female. You just don't know it yet."

His eyes told her he was about to enlighten her.

"You're ready, Sunny," he said, his voice husking sensually. "Maybe you don't feel ready up here—" he touched her forehead "—but you are ready."

Erotic fingers fanned across her lips and eased along the curve of her throat. "You're ready here—" snaking down over soft velour, they sketched a vibrant line along the sensitive outer swell of her breast "—and here."

A thrill grabbed low and hard as he began to slowly unzip the length of her jacket. His voice tightened with desire. "Here," he said, tracing the soft cleft between her breasts. "And especially here—" fingers trailed toward her midriff, circling her navel and then wending toward—

Her muscles jerked sharply. A fist clutched in her stomach. "No," she breathed, pushing his hand away. "No, I'm not ready there—"

He hesitated, studied her with darkening eyes. A waver of sympathetic irony touched his lips. "Oh, Sunny, you're so ready there it hurts, doesn't it?"

Heat scorched her cheeks. "Yes," she admitted. He shifted toward her and she hunched protectively. "I mean, yes it hurts, not yes, I'm ready."

For a flickering second, he halted, almost smiled. And then his eyes strayed back to her open jacket, her exposed breasts. Startled, she watched a raw shudder of emotion move through his features. His body visibly tensed. Abruptly, he was deadly serious, a man in need.

His breath punctured the air. His hand circled her wrists and tugged gently. "Listen to me," he said, a roughness fraying the edges of his control. "I know you're frightened, Sunny, but sometimes we're afraid of what we want most."

He pressed her hand between his, brought her fingertips to his lips. "God, I want this night with you—so damn badly, I can't think straight anymore." A soft growl rumbled in his throat as his mouth found her palm. The shimmer of his lips over sensitive skin nearly made her gasp.

His breathing harshened. His hand slipped to her wrist and he pulled her closer. "I'm running out of willpower, Sunny. I'm a man, I want a woman. I want you."

Her heart raced like a frightened animal, a trapped animal. She met his eyes and felt a shock wave of awareness.

He wouldn't, *couldn't* wait any longer. His drives were too strong. He was fighting demons and losing. They lit his eyes, burned through his steel control. She turned away, shaken.

"Be with me, Sunny," he whispered, his voice straining. "Give in to it . . . take the risk."

Oh God, he *was* a risk, she realized, trembling, the biggest risk of her life. He was asking her to walk the tightrope without a safety net. He'd never said he loved her, never promised her more than just one night. He'd made it clear he wanted her with no strings, no bargains.

He brought her head around, and she looked into eyes so blue they hurt her with their brilliance. "It has to be your choice."

Her lips parted to tell him she wanted him, but the high, painful racing of her heart silenced her. As she stared up at his taut, expectant face, a startling truth flooded her awareness. *She was in love with this man.*

A sharp pain claimed her heart. The realization left her so vulnerable, so exposed she began to tremble. She'd really believed that passion was enough, that an affair, even a night with him was enough, but it wasn't, *it wasn't.* A premonition coursed through her. If he left her, *if he didn't love her,* it would shatter her.

"Sunny?"

Dropping her gaze, she saw the crushed orchid in her hands. Anguished, unable to speak, she shook her head.

She heard his dragged-in-breath, heard him almost audibly wrench himself under control . . . heard him turn and walk to the door.

Tears of frustration dried on her face as Sunny ran across the hotel's private beach to the ocean. She halted in the glittering darkness, retying her bikini top, shuddering as a wave crested high and crashed down with a thunderous sound. She squeezed her eyes shut, fighting a dread of the ocean she'd had since childhood.

With a tight cry, she dashed out into the surf like a mad woman, splashing in up to her waist, diving just as the next wave broke.

She came up on the other side, spluttering sprays of water, treading hard and frantically. The heavy swells buoyed her up, rocked her off her feet. Another wave caught her, spun her around and carried her back to shore. She rode with its pommeling force, landed on the beach in a flailing, breathless collision with the sand.

Gasping, crying, pulling herself out of the water, she felt a sudden tremor and nearly doubled over. A small, sharp cry ripped through her as she felt the full impact of the emotions she'd been holding in. They hit her like a blow. She loved him, she needed him, *she had to be with him no matter what the risk.*

If a brief affair, even if one night was all she had, then she'd take it, grab for it with both hands.

She sprang up, shaking, running toward the hotel, angry at herself for not realizing it before, angry at him for...well for something, dammit—even if she wasn't quite sure what.

Alone and dripping in the pool elevator, she regretted running out without a cover-up, or even a towel.

The doors opened on the sixth floor, her floor.

She shut her eyes and hung onto the railing, waiting for it to slide shut. Her mind flashed an image of a race-car without brakes, it's driver forced to watch herself careen toward a magnificent catastrophe. When the doors rolled open again at seven, she hesitated, then walked automatically to where her room would have been on that floor and knocked, praying she had the right one. Her heart in her throat, she waited, sleek, dripping, her feet in a puddle of Pacific Ocean water.

He was tying his robe as he opened the door.

She felt the surprised sweep of his blue eyes as if he were physically touching her. "Hi?" she ventured, managing a shaky smile and a little wave.

The shock in his features softened, and his eyes melted to a warm radiance as he took in her mermaid state. "Did you come to borrow a towel?" he asked, a telling hoarseness in his voice.

"Oh, Gray," she murmured, trembling, blinking. A tear pushed over and rolled down her cheek. Before it could fall from her chin, she was in his arms.

"Sunny," he groaned, holding her, lifting her off the ground to swing her around. "God, you're a miracle." He set her down, brushed a damp tendril from her face. "I've never met a woman who kept me so off balance. I never know what to expect."

"Look who's talking." She laughed, a soft, shrill sound from the heart.

Never taking his eyes from her, he reached behind her, pushed the door shut and flipped the lock. "You're mine, now," he warned her, engagingly gruff. His hand cupped the back of her head, drawing her toward him. "No backing out, no changing your mind?"

"Never," she vowed bravely, meeting his eyes. A soft ache whispered through her, making her want to wriggle with pleasure. Instead, she eased closer and trailed a trembling finger through the sun streaked hair that feathered over his ear. "I've come to offer myself up for your pleasure, sir," she whispered, startled at her own boldness.

His eyes darkened. "Keep saying things like that and you'll make me forget that I want to make this the best thing that's ever happened to you."

She smiled, secretly thrilled that she'd shaken his control. Her fingers found his lips, slipped along their textured edge.

"You know what you're doing to me, don't you?" he moaned. He caught her hand, stepped back and looked at the beads of water shivering on her skin. "Come on, mermaid, let's dry you off."

Smothering waves of trepidation, she let herself be led into the bathroom.

He picked up a huge, fluffy towel and turned to look at her, his eyes becoming a light caress that sensitized her body everywhere they touched. "You're a dangerous weapon in that bathing suit," he said, huskily, lightly blotting the remaining water from her face.

He eased the towel along her throat and shoulders and down her arms. Her breath caught as he patted the taut, flushed area above her bikini bra and then moved down to her midriff.

She felt a trembling in her legs as he worked his way down, lifting first one foot then the other to thoroughly dry them. "Turn around," he said finally.

She did, her stomach muscles contracting spontaneously. Within her, an erotic string formed a knot that coiled tighter with every stroke of the towel. Her instinctive fears were giving way to something heated, wonderful... primal.

She felt him lingering on her lower back, felt the terry cloth gentling over tensed buttocks with deliberate pressure. Without warning, his finger ran a vivid tracer along the high-cut line of her bikini. In its wake, she felt tingly starstreams of heat, like a thousand fireflies touching down on her skin. Oh God, he was doing such terrible things to her insides.

"You're still wet under the bathing suit," he informed her, his finger dipping beneath the stretchy fabric.

"Yes," she said, trying to catch her breath. "I am."

"Maybe I'd better do something about that."

She wavered, caught herself unsteadily. "Maybe you'd better."

As he began to ease the bikini bottom down, she felt deep muscles contract with a lightning bolt of sensation. The alarm inside her began to flash *point of no return*! "Gray," she said tremulously, catching his hand. "Wait, please. I'm

not changing my mind or anything, but perhaps, well...
shouldn't we talk or something, first. I mean about our—"

The bikini bottom stopped its descent. "Talk?"

Don't say it, you coward. She dropped her head, sighed
and mumbled, "Yeah, about our...relationship, the—"

"Future?" he finished for her, turning her around.

It was a long moment before she could look up at him,
and when she did she saw something new in his features, an
enigmatic grace, a simple element of truth that made her
stare and search and want to have it for her own.

Unyielding, he pressed his hands along her jawline. "I
know your background dictates that I should have promised you the moon and the stars by now, but don't make me
seduce you with promises. What I can give you is so much
better than that. I'm asking you to share yourself, Sunny,
right now, in this moment. And I'm offering you everything I have—*myself.* Please let that be enough."

She shut her eyes and nodded. "Yes," she whispered, exhaling all the air in her lungs. *"Yes."* It was enough,
enough, oh God, it felt like a gift.

Bending down, she picked up the towel.

As he took it from her, their eyes met and held.

She saw the raw need in him, felt it open her like a late-
blooming flower. "Yes," she whispered again and again, her
hands shaking so hard she could barely loosen the ties of her
bikini top. As the bra fell away, its strings clung to her damp
skin.

Aware of his clenched jar, his sucked-in breath, she shook
herself free, her breasts shimmering in a soft, wanton response to her movements.

"Perhaps you'd better finish drying me?" she offered, her
voice a silky tremor.

As he touched the towel to her breasts, she felt the need
of him so profoundly, so deeply it seemed to cry out from
the marrow of her bones.

Nine

Gray saw the naked longing in her eyes, felt a physical snap of sexuality hit him like a whiplash. A groan hissed through his teeth. He dropped the towel, cupped the swell of her breasts with his hands. Their silky heat tortured his control. "I want you now, Sunny, right here," he told her, his jaw flexing like twisted steel. "But we're going to take this slow, make it right."

She nodded, her eyes bright and feverish.

He eased curled fingers down her stomach and a blushing wake of sexual desire radiated out from the path he created.

Her whimper nearly destroyed him.

"Oh, Sunny," he whispered. His hands locked over the curve of her hipbones, bringing her to him. Their loins met with swift, urgent pressure, her soft body arousing his maleness to the point of pain.

A groaning tension erupted from him in soft, harsh laughter. "My grand plan isn't working, Sunny. I wanted to touch you, love you slowly, bring our fantasies alive. But, God help me, you're wilder than any fantasy." His hands framed her face, rocking it to and fro with roughened tenderness, then he combed his fingers into her hair. "I've waited so long."

"Gray," she whispered, insinuating her body against his with a searing little thrust of her hips. "I'm ready—I want you, too. Here—" she told him softly, guiding his fingers over budding nipples, down over her stomach, easing them inside her bikini bottom "—and here."

She nearly cried out as his fingers discovered her silky depths. Arching against his hand, she breathed, "I need you, Gray, I need you so bad it hurts. Make love to me, *now*."

Her urgent demand stripped him of all control. Tugging the bikini bottom off her, he swept her up and carried her to the bed.

As he fought free of his bathrobe, she moaned, rolled away from him and curled into a sensuous ball. The sight of her creamy skin spurred him to a near explosion of desire. He drew in air, clenched his fists, cooling, cooling his ardor.

After a long, tense moment, he touched her hip and she rolled back, opening her arms to him. Her long pale beauty nearly cut off his breathing. He knelt over her, inhaled her heated scent, caressed her lips with his.

Breaking off with a tight moan, he feathered his hands down her trembling body, spreading her legs as he eased back up.

Her body tensed, its surface musculature rigid beneath his caress. Not from fear, he realized. She awaited him, eyes darkening with a breathless invitation.

With a muffled groan, he lifted his weight over her, centering his hips in the soft saddle of her thighs.

"Gray," she breathed, heavy-lidded eyes searching his face. "This is our first time." Her hushed voice caught.

"That means everything's new again, doesn't it? We're new, you and I?"

A resonance brushed his heart. "Yes," he said huskily. Yes, he felt new with her, felt all the urgency of the very first time. Energy pulsed low and hard. He shifted, sought, felt his rigid flesh come into contact with her thigh. Her body shuddered, almost spasmed.

"Easy, easy," he soothed, fighting for control. "It's okay, Sunny, I'll take it slow—" The words broke off, unintelligible as he found the entry to her searing warmth. The hard ache of desire shot through him.

Their gaze connected, held as he moved against her, testing her narrow enclosure. With each questing probe, she whimpered, arching, wrapping legs and arms around him.

"I need you," he told her, caressing her face with kisses, "need to be inside you." He eased into her carefully, curbing a fierce instinct to thrust, to take possession. Her body's resistance baffled him. How long had it been for her? She was tight, too tight—rigid with fear, desire? He had to release those taut muscles or he'd hurt her.

Shifting his weight to one side, he skimmed his palm along her soft curves to the heat between her thighs and found the moist, budding softness.

His jaw clenched in a spasm as he explored her petalled silk. "Yes, there?" he asked in response to her sharp inhalation. He kept the pressure light, tantalizing, and when she began to undulate and strain against him, he entered her with his fingers.

The velvet enclosure incited his sex to sweet throbbing contractions. Her breathless pleadings made his heart surge painfully.

He pulled free, moving above her again. "Oh, yes," he moaned as her heat opened up to him, gradually, taking him, sheathing him in exquisite fluttering warmth. A slow groaning wonder tightened his facial muscles as he moved into her, fighting the urge to plunge too deeply, uncontrollably.

"Gray," she murmured, her face flushed with color. Slender fingers dug into his flanks.

Go easy, he warned himself, bring her along slowly. But her sensual murmurings and urgent movements spurred him to faster, deeper strokes.

Shuddering, he drove into her, heard her shocked cry. "Am I hurting you?" he rasped.

"No, no—I want you," she entreated, her hands gripping his hips, desperation in her voice as she ran her fingers up his straining body, entangling them in his hair. "Please, *please*, I want you. I want it all."

With a racking moan, he buried himself in her enveloping fire. Their bodies merged like a vital force, a shattering release of passion connecting them. Crying, gasping, they rocked and clashed, clinging, coupling with primitive, driving rhythms.

With a shuddering half-sob, Sunny surrendered to the passion vibrating through her body. She flung her arms out, and Gray captured them, dragging them above her head. Her hips strained against him, moving with instinctual need, coaxing him, enticing him until he thrust into her, filling her with a force that jarred the breath from her body.

"You're beautiful," he vowed, his broken whispers caressing her lips, "as free as a wild animal."

He shifted slightly to kiss her throat. Sensing he meant to pull back, she wrenched her hands free of his grasp. *"No,"* she breathed, desperate, her fingers coiling in his hair. All her muscles contracted, straining to hold him, to keep him deep inside her. And then he was moving, pressing into her again, filling her with such sweet, sharp joy.

A searing pleasure ribboned through her, its intensity beyond anything she'd ever felt or imagined. Suddenly, inexplicably, her heart expanded with such a swell of emotion that tears blurred her eyes. *She loved him.*

His roughened moan bathed her senses, and a soaring excitement took her as he breathed her name. "Sunny," he exhaled again and again, holding her face, enclosing her in the aura of his whisper-harsh voice.

She could sense that he moved instinctively now, unchecked. Each thrust incited her to trembling, high-pitched sounds that shocked and aroused her. Excitement pierced her with knifelike strokes of pleasure. "Gray," she whispered desperately, feeling unbearable pressures build, "don't stop, don't ever stop."

Her whole body shuddered convulsively as he crushed her to him. Gasping, she felt a jet stream of pleasure sweep through her, pleasure so exquisite it stormed the gateway of ecstasy. And then, in a stunning flurry of movement, Gray's deep strokes broke through the gateway to send her spiraling toward the stars.

For an eternity of seconds, a crescendo of light and sensation and sound flooded her. Lost in radiant shimmers, she felt her body gripping him, spasming around him, felt a brilliant pulse radiating from their union.

She heard his breath catch with a sharp concussive gasp. He forced out her name, *"Sunny."* And then ecstasy took him. Gripping her with brutal strength, he bucked once, twice, his body shuddering with pleasure.

She clung to him, gasping softly as a ripple of completion ran through their joined bodies in one continuous wave. And then she went limp, utterly limp, as though her bones had melted.

The world hovered in another dimension as she lay beneath him, vaguely conscious, bathing in his quiet shudders, savoring the feel of his weight . . . reveling in his husky murmurs of love.

Love? A tiny moué of completion curved her lips and spread until her entire body smiled. Yes . . . *love*. Just listen. In the tangled aftermath of their union, she felt and heard a barely discernable timbre caressing them as their bodies hummed the honeyed chant of warmed limbs and resting pulses. With a radiant sigh, she stretched and absorbed his body's whispers of love and adoration.

As he withdrew to lie beside her, she snuggled against him, resting her head in the hollow of his shoulder. They lay there for a time, drifting in and out of waking dreams and lazily shared bliss.

Rousing finally, Sunny sighed contentedly, and with her forefinger began making wistful designs in the thick dusting of his chest hair.

A little aftershock moved through him in a long shuddering exhalation. "And to think," he said, his laughter laced with wonder and emotion, "that I was worried about you."

She smiled, murmured, "I beg your pardon?"

He rolled to his side, rested his chin against his fist. "*You* are a mind-blowing experience." Capturing a lock of shiny blond hair, he rubbed it between his thumb and forefinger. "I'd modestly planned to be the man to desensitize your inhibitions, to set free the passion in your nature."

"You did," she assured him, her eyes sparkling. "I've never felt like that before, *never*. I was so high—" she looked over her shoulder at the starlit sky "—I was floating out there somewhere. Out there trailing my toes in the Milky Way."

"Sunny," he said, a soberness shadowing his voice. "I'm going to ask you a question. You don't have to answer—"

She came around quickly. "What is it?"

He rested a protective hand along the extended line of her throat. "You and Ted? You were intimate, weren't you? Lovers?"

She felt herself coloring and looked away. "Yes...of course. It's just that...well, with Ted's being on the East Coast and my being here it was difficult—" She shrugged. "You know what I mean, a bicoastal relationship, two careers and all." She broke off then, aware that the rationalizations she'd used for years were really excuses. "The truth," she confessed, glancing up, "is that I avoided sex. Ted wasn't, well ..." Trailing off, she admitted another truth. "I always thought it was me, that I didn't inspire him, that I wasn't the lusty type."

Gray's eyebrows quirked at that. He ran a finger over her mouth, replaced it with his lips and murmured, "We just shot the hell out of that theory."

"Yup," she agreed, laughing, snuggling into him. "We're quite a research team, aren't we? Maybe we'll give Masters and Johnson a run for their money." Her eyes lit. "Hey, that could require considerable ... experimentation."

His eyes sparkled. "From a novice to a sexual researcher in one night? She's making remarkable progress."

"Novice, Doc? I think I'm offended. I'd preferred to categorize myself as unaroused and unfulfilled—until now."

His breath of laughter ruffled her hair. "I'd categorize you as the best thing that's ever happened to a man."

The promise in his voice made her blink. "Really?" she said softly, leaning back to look up at him. "Anybody I know?"

He met her eyes, exhaled and then retreated like an uncertain suitor. "Hey," he said, grinning boyishly. "It's a beautiful night and it's ours. Let's do something, go for a walk, go swimming—"

"I've been swimming," she reminded him.

"A walk then." He moved lithely around her, pushed off the bed, as naked as the original Adam, and offered her his hands. "Come on, you can make it as far as the patio door."

She blinked and blushed. Lord, what a build. *Major everything*. Suddenly shy, she glanced down, saw her own nakedness, grabbed for the bedspread and wrapped it around her like a sarong.

He tried to squelch a grin and failed. "Cold?"

When she nodded, he sat down beside her, a counselor-at-large expression on his face. "Hey, lady, you've come too far tonight to start hiding inside bedspreads." He gave the material she'd clutched around her a gentle yank.

She yanked back. "Give the lady a break, counselor. She's having an attack of the bashfuls, okay?"

His eyes brightened to a dizzying blue. "Umm... unpredictable. One minute she's sexy, the next she's shy. But, that's okay. I love it." He caught her, rolled her back on the bed and slung a long leg over her.

Pressed into the mattress by his weight, she stared up at him, instantly aware that despite all they'd shared, his sexual intensity still sent shivers of apprehension through her.

He pressed his lips to her bare shoulder, then touched his tongue to the corner of her mouth, giving her a lovely little jolt.

"I've got a great idea," he said. "I'll open the wine I ordered from room service and we'll take it out on the lanai. Loan me half of your bedspread?"

She quickly decided it would be safer to share her cover with him than let him stroll around in the buff. Their neighbors might not be ready for a naked talk-show host.

With much bumping, jostling and laughter, he was wrapped up. They found a glass in the bathroom, took the wine in its plastic bucket of melted ice and made it out to the lanai.

They bundled onto a chaise lounge, knees, elbows and hipbones touching. Gray, looking equal parts sexy and ridiculous, made a sober ritual of opening the wine, checking its color and bouquet, then sniffing the cork.

"What if someone sees us?" Sunny said, giggling as she swigged from the bathroom tumbler full of Chablis.

"I can see it on the newsstands now." His hand made a short arc in the air between them. "Hosts Of *Esprit* Cavort Naked And Drunk In Hawaii."

"And they'd be right for once," she said, laughing, passing him the glass.

"Forget the media," he said extravagantly. "Tonight calls for a toast."

"Oh yes." She inhaled, expectant.

He held up their only glass. "Odysseys to the Milky Way. May we have many, many more."

Her held breath came out in a disappointed, "Oh."

"Not a good toast?" He looked perplexed.

She shrugged, avoiding his eyes. "It was fine—just not what I had in mind."

Golden eyebrows slanted, full of wary mischief. "Care to tell me what that might have been?"

"Something more ... meaningful."

He went back to looking perplexed. Sunny felt a ping of annoyance. She knew exactly what she was getting at. Why didn't he? "I thought you psychologists were supposed to be sensitive, intuitive," she muttered reproachfully.

"Ex-psychologist," he reminded her. "I haven't had a clinical practice for years. Listen, I'm sorry but my intuitive skills are a little blunted at the moment." He put the half-empty tumbler in the bucket alongside the wine bottle and grinned at her. "So what's cooking in that unpredictable noggin of yours? I have a feeling it's something I'm supposed to know, right?" He rubbed his chin thoughtfully. "How about a clue. Is it a song title?"

Damn, she wanted so badly to take back her bedspread!

She looked squarely into confident eyes. "If you ask me if it's bigger than a bread box, I swear I'll—" Okay, he wanted a clue, she'd give him a clue. "I happen to be crazy in love with you, Graham Chance," she said, her voice cracking with emotion. "I want to know exactly what that means to you. I want to know how you feel about me."

He froze for an instant, did a slow take of amazement, then began to shake his head. "You shoot straight from the hip, don't you?"

Pressing fingers to her lips, she merely stared back at him. God, there was something wonderful, something so *liberating* about saying exactly what you felt.

Gray remained quiet, studying her for the longest time, so long her quick fix of exhilaration changed to worry. Was he trying to figure out how to reject her? Was there someone else? Kristin? No, she would not make the mistake of asking about that woman again.

"Well?" she prompted, unable to stand the pressure a minute longer. Forcing the nervous husk from her voice, she said, "A certain blond talk-show host from L.A. is waiting for an answer."

An odd energy lurked behind Gray's serious expression. Sunny felt her heart jump as he finally spoke.

"I have it on good authority," he averred quietly, "that the talk-show host in question is shy, sexy... *very brave*." His blue eyes dazzled her. "And she claims to be a Gemini, my favorite sign." A slow-glowing smile touched his lips. "What's not to love?"

He reached out to touch her cheek, and the tenderness in his caress sent a delighted shiver through her. The warmth in his smile and the look in his eyes made her wonder if she'd died and gone to heaven. This, she thought rapturously, is the look of a man smitten. No, *a man in love.*

She sighed and all around her the fragrant darkness came alive with the promise of early summer; its breezes whispered out secret wishes, soft yearnings. Above them, stars studded the night sky with twinkling crystal chandeliers of light.

Gray's deepening smile reached for her heart. "What's not to love?" he repeated softly.

An aura of sheer exhuberant joy enveloped her as he pushed away folds of bedspread and pulled her into his arms.

"This way quickly!" the young woman urged, beckoning Gray and Sunny out of the limo and toward a side entrance that led to the Hilo Airport terminals. A group of security guards preceded her.

"We'll bypass most of the crowds this way," the airport rep explained, "not to mention reporters. Our security people spotted some at the front entrance."

As they rushed down the corridor, Gray took Sunny's hand and squeezed it. The quick smile they exchanged brimmed with unspoken meaning.

The young woman whirled around nimbly, walking backward for a few quick steps. "We're holding up United's connecting flight to Kennedy for you, Mr. Chance..."

Sunny felt a wistful pull. The week in Hawaii had gone too quickly. Now Gray was on his way to New York to jockey an anniversary special for his former radio station, and she was on her way back to L.A. to tape interviews for next week's shows.

"And Ms. Tyler?" the woman was saying. "We have you on Hawaiian Airline's flight to LAX."

Sunny nodded, dropping Gray's hand as they reached double doors and were ushered out into the typical airport chaos of waiting tourists and traveling businessmen.

"Right this way," the airport rep directed, clearing a path.

"Sunny!" a voice called.

"Damn," Gray muttered, taking her elbow protectively as a pack of reporters moved toward them.

"When's the wedding?" one of the reporters yelled.

The airport rep waved them away. "Please, no questions now."

"What's the nature of your relationship?" another one asked, pushing through to walk beside Sunny.

"We're friends," Gray said unpleasantly. "Want me to spell that for you?"

"Intimate friends?" a third jeered.

The frozen lift of Gray's chin caused Sunny to grab his shirt-sleeve. *"Don't,"* she whispered, hoping that one succinct word would cover whatever he had in mind.

By the time they reached Gray's terminal, a huge curious group had collected behind them.

"I'll see you in a few days," Gray said, searching Sunny's face, obviously wanting to say things he couldn't under the circumstances.

"Dedicate a song to me, promise?" she whispered. "Something mushy?"

He laughed and nodded his head.

"Mr. Chance?" the airport rep urged, taking his arm.

"I've got to go," he told Sunny regretfully, backing up the ramp. "One song coming up," he said, waving just before he disappeared from sight.

She waved back, embarrassed by the tears that suddenly blurred her eyes. Cameras clicked as she hurried away to her own plane.

Midflight to Los Angeles, Sunny finally managed to relax. What a week she'd had. The greatest love of her life and the biggest show of her career had proved to be an exhilarating and exhausting combination.

On an impulse, she took a publicity photo of her and Gray from her bag and gazed at it. Her smile became a sappy grin. Gray looked straight back at her, unsmiling, all bronzed angles and classy blue-eyed temperament. Yes sir, she thought, resisting the urge to salute. A tight little hum vibrated clear to her toes. Was he the most gorgeous man on either side of the continental divide, or was she just a little bit biased?

"Your diet Coke." A stewardess set the drink on the tray next to Sunny's seat.

"Thanks," she murmured, embarrassed to be caught with such a blissful expression on her face.

"Your new show is fabulous," the stewardess bubbled eagerly. "I know it's going to be a big hit. You and Gray are *so* good together."

Sunny beamed and thanked her. So good together is right, she thought, glancing out the window and wondering how she was going to get through the next few days without him.

They'd taped extra shows in Hawaii in order to free Gray to emcee the anniversary special. His radio talk show's widespread appeal had generated something of a cult following in the two years he'd been there, and the clamor to have him back had convinced the RBC brass it would be good publicity.

But Gray had mentioned something about other business to take care of in New York as well, which meant she would be deprived of his company for four whole days. Would she survive? Not a chance. She'd be chin-deep in withdrawal pangs by tonight.

She laid her head back, staring off into space. Courage, she reminded herself. She would have to hold body and soul together through tomorrow anyway. There were two interview tapings to be done and a posh black-tie party tomorrow evening.

An involuntary shudder caught her by surprise. Somehow, all her notoriety had bounced her up from the wine-and-cheese crowd to coveted A-List status. It wasn't that she didn't like parties, but an A party sounded like hard work. Especially when the host was Rudolph Grant, the conglomerate king whose automobile parts franchises were one of *Esprit*'s biggest sponsors.

She took a sip of her diet Coke. How did one conduct oneself at such a prestigious affair? All of these elite, in-crowd functions had their own private protocol. Yee gods, she thought, her lips freezing on the rim of the glass. What did she really know about Hollywood's *inner* circle? What was Sunny Tyler doing wading into the deep waters of Hollywood society?

Confidence, she told herself firmly, you've got the right stuff. She felt a sudden giddy flash of impending luck, as though her new relationship with Gray had brought her to a special state of grace where absolutely nothing could go wrong!

She took a generous swig of her diet Coke and considered ordering something stronger. Who was it that said "if everything's coming your way, you must be standing in the wrong lane"? She rolled her eyes. Such a killjoy.

Ten

Sunny scrutinized herself in one of the powder room's elaborate gilt stucco wall mirrors and sucked in a tummy-minimizing breath. Was there anything to be done about this dress? she wondered. The frothy white Roland Jones original loaned to her from RBC's wardrobe department fit beautifully. Too beautifully? The new Merry Widow design that had seemed so stylishly daring in her bedroom mirror now looked like something that should have stayed in her underwear drawer.

The muted rustlings and tinklings of the elegant party outside reminded her that if she hid in the ladies' room any longer she'd be committing yet another faux pas this evening.

The first mistake had been arriving at this black tie affair alone. A fierce bout of stomach flu had felled Steve at the last minute, and when Sunny called to make their excuses to the host, he'd insisted she come anyway. On her arrival, the flutter of curious glances had alerted her that she was flaunting party etiquette.

Not an auspicious start for her A-List debut.

Her second mistake of the evening glared at her from the mirror. A designer dress that looked like a funky corset.

"Can I help, ma'am?" a maid inquired, hovering.

"No, thanks," Sunny said, tugging the strapless top up a bit. Her modest breasts positively overflowed the snug-fitting bodice. She'd never felt so voluptuous. No deep breaths in this thing, she reminded herself, or you'll be flashing the cream of Hollywood society.

She sighed carefully and looked at the gilded door that would take her down a velvet-paneled hallway and back into the most tastefully sumptuous party she'd ever had the nerve-racking good fortune to attend. Smile your heart out, she reminded herself, with one last wistful glance in the mirror.

Steve's pep talk came back to her. "Get used to it, Sunshine. You've achieved celebrity status now, and this elite bash goes with the territory."

The maid had the door open well before she reached it. "Thank you," Sunny murmured, unused to such wholesale pampering.

She hesitated outside, looking up and down the narrow hallway. Since the party occupied the entire first floor of Rudolph Grant's pseudo-French country chateau, she had several options. The architect must have had Versailles in mind when he conceived this place, she decided.

To her right, a grand reception room boasted buffet tables, well-stocked bars and mouth-watering scents. To her left, a salon decorated in shades of peach and cream held groups of quiet conversationalists, and beyond that rococo French doors opened onto a ballroom with high-gloss hardwood floors where an orchestra played vaguely Latin rhythms and a Julio Iglesias look-alike crooned an incoherent ballad.

A footman in white and gold braid hustled down the hallway to offer his arm. "Shall I escort *mademoiselle* back?"

Not knowing quite how to refuse, she nodded, and quickly decided on the salon. Left at the doorway, she searched for someone who looked even slightly approachable. A well-known scion of the fashion industry looked her way, smiled and nodded as he took in the Roland Jones gown.

His arched smile held interest, she realized nervously. Was it the dress he was looking at...or the woman about to spill out of it?

"What's shakin'?" a male voice inquired. Sunny's gaze came around to see Neil Butler, a young film director approaching her. One of Hollywood's new breed of hands-on filmmakers, the shambling, bearded auteur looked as out of place as she felt.

"You solo, too?" he asked.

"Yes," Sunny said, grateful for even this rather incongruous kindred spirit.

"Why don't we split before these sleepwalkers start somnambulating into dinner?" He moved closer, said under his breath, "Heard of the Hard Rock Café? They've got an act there I'm thinking of putting in my next film. Wanna check it out?"

"Oh, thank you, but I don't think—" Startled Sunny saw their host, Rudolph Grant, coming their way, flanked by the dress designer and someone she instantly recognized as the woman who'd hung all over Gray at the RBC party—Madeline Downs.

The auto-parts king acknowledged Butler with a nod. "And you, Miss Tyler?" he asked almost rhetorically. "Are you enjoying yourself?'' He made brusque introductions all around.

"Ummm, yes, Sunny Tyler," Madeline murmured, green eyes glinting. "Such an interesting dress. It looks exactly like the Roland Jones the studio had made for my guest spot on *Texas*." Her eyes dropped to Sunny's bodice before lifting to flutter fetchingly at their host. "Though I'm afraid I didn't carry it off with such . . . abandon."

A surprised rush of color heated Sunny's cheeks. She was still trying to think of a fitting response when a footman appeared on the landing. "Dinner is served."

"I'll drop my plate on her at dinner," Butler promised Sunny as they filed into a huge dining room. "Hey, maybe we'll get a food fight going?"

Sunny instantly vetoed the idea despite its perverse appeal.

Dinner was an eight-course extravaganza of French haute cuisine that kept Sunny busy choosing the right crystal and silverware. By dessert she'd gone through half a dozen forks—and seriously endangered the hand-finished seams of her dress.

With the last plates spirited away, the gentlemen took their cigars and brandy while the ladies dutifully retired to freshen up.

A little dizzy from all the fine wines and stuffy glamour, Sunny sank onto a silk damask chair, grateful to have the ladies' room to herself. She'd barely taken a breath when the door swung open and Madeline Downs wafted in.

"Sunny, what fun to see you, again," the actress tittered, as though it had been years. "Now that I have you alone, you must tell me the truth. What do you think of all this scandalous behind-the-scenes business? Were you in on it, too, dear?"

"In? On what?"

Madeline looked undisguisedly smug. "Steve Freedkin's brainstorm to boost ratings. That man is a wizard at commercial hype," she volunteered conspiratorially, "but he's overstepped himself this time."

Sunny straightened, wary. "What do you mean?"

The actress's smile revealed a blinding flash of teeth. "You don't know?" She pulled a folded newspaper article from her sequined bag. "This came out today. I heard you'd be here, so I brought the article along. According to this, Steve engineered all those sizzling romance rumors about you and Gray. He even made a deal with this scandal sheet to print them—"

"What?" Stunned, Sunny stared at the paper, unable to take it from the actress's hand. "Those tabloids are full of lies," she countered, her voice thin. "Everybody knows that."

Madeline's outstretched arm never wavered.

Swallowing nervously, Sunny took the paper and began to skim the newsprint.

"Their editor says they have proof—taped telephone conversations between Steve and their publicist."

"Tapes can be fixed," Sunny retorted, glancing up. "And even if it is true, so what? It's not an uncommon practice in this town to create scandals for some instant publicity."

Somewhere in her heart, Sunny knew Steve would be quite capable of such a thing. That he'd resorted to it distressed her, but not nearly as much as the article's next insinuation.

Beneath her fingers a paragraph stated, "An inside source reports that Graham Chance agreed to go along with the romance publicity to boost the show's ratings. Chance was overheard telling Freedkin that Sunny Tyler wasn't his type, but he'd play along. The source says Chance was motivated by the network brass's interest in *L.A. Heartbeat*."

Sunny's hands began to tremble. She felt sick inside. Her overwrought nerves reacted as though every word were true.

"Interesting reading, isn't it?" Madeline inquired. The actress turned toward the mirror and fluffed her hair. "You'll excuse me?" she murmured, moving toward the gold-fixtured rest room. "It must be all that wine." Unable to resist a parting smirk, she closed the small room's door and clicked the lock.

Crushing the article in her hands, Sunny reminded herself that these papers made a living out of lies and innuendo.

"None of this is true," she whispered, standing. She whisked up her purse to leave, took two jerky steps and hesitated, staring at the bathroom door.

Biting back an urge to rap on it and tell the woman inside what she could do with her article, she swung around to leave. One step from the door an inspired idea halted her in her tracks. There were ways to deal with the Madeline Downs of this world. Did she dare?

"Not in a million years," she mumbled under her breath. No sane person would consider such a perverse—

Glancing around, she saw no maid in residence. A nervous giggle bubbled. An instant later, she sprinted into action.

Her fingers trembling, she borrowed a metal nail file from one of the gilded toiletry trays and carefully loosened the screws that held the bathroom door's ornate knob in place. When she tried it gingerly, the knob on her side dropped out and clunked to the carpeting.

With a dark smile, Sunny tapped lightly.

"It's occupied," Madeline called.

"It certainly is," Sunny agreed. "And it will be for quite some time."

"Pardon me?" Madeline called again.

"Not a chance," Sunny muttered, scribbling an Out of Order sign on a scrap of paper and affixing it to the outer door as she left. *There*. They might not find her for hours, days!

On her way back to the salon, she happened onto Butler, the young filmmaker, bidding their austere host goodbye.

"I'm afraid I must leave, too," she said regretfully, shaking Rudolph Grant's hand. "I can't think when I've had such a deeply satisfying evening. We must do this again."

"Real soon," Butler chimed in dryly.

As their host hustled away, Sunny and the director exchanged a quick, conspiratorial look. "Can I drop you somewhere?" he asked, grinning.

"As a matter of fact, you can," she said quietly, hooking his arm. "There's someone I need to see, fast."

The trip to Steve's apartment in Marina Del Rey was a wincing, white-knuckle experience. Butler had taken her literally. To her dismay, she also discovered that he harbored great hostility for both the D.M.V. and the California traffic code. "Oppressive Facist dogma," he mumbled, making an illegal left turn.

But not even legitimate fear for life and limb could take Sunny's mind off the article in her purse. By the time they reached Steve's apartment, she'd managed to convince herself that the scandal sheets had fabricated another enormous lie.

"Want me to wait?" Butler offered, pulling to the curb. Sunny quickly shook her head, thanked him for the ride and let herself out. Preoccupied, she started for Steve's building.

The Roll's window swooshed down. "Hell of a dress," he called, grinning as he leaned over. "Look me up if you ever get tired of television. I'll put you in the movies." Saluting, he executed a U-turn through screeching brakes and honking horns, and drove off.

Sunny hurried past a snoring guard at the gate. Surprised to find the door to Steve's apartment unlocked, she let herself in and called out, "Yoo-hoo."

"In here," Steve moaned from the bedroom. His greenish tinged face peered out at her from underneath the bed covers as she entered. "Oh, it's you," he said weakly. "I thought you were Mrs. Schwartz, my neighbor, with the chicken soup."

Sunny pulled the crumpled article from her bag, determined not to show sympathy until he'd absolved himself. "Explain this, please," she requested, smoothing the paper out and handing it to him.

"What now?" With feeble indignation, he shook his head. "Sunny, can't you see I'm sick, terminal? Leave a dying man in peace."

"Read it," she ordered with the severity of a drill sergeant.

One eye shut, he took it, reading painfully. His expression faded from green to ashen.

Sunny's sick feeling came hurtling back. She sank to the edge of the bed.

The article slipped from Steve's hand and floated to the floor. "What do you want me to say?" he asked quietly.

"You can tell me how it's a pack of lies—" desperation crept into her voice "—and how you're going to ask RBC's legal team to sue."

"I can't do that."

"Why not?"

His shoulders lifted. "Because they've got it right. It's all true." Rallying briefly, he warned, "And don't ask me to apologize. I did it for the show, and I'd do it again."

"Steve," she said, quietly horrified. "You can't play God with people's lives like that. Those rumors hurt Ted. Look what they did to our engagement."

"For that you should thank me," he insisted, his voice gathering some strength. "My God, Sunny, you might have married that guy."

At her incredulous stare, he backed off. "Okay—maybe thanks is too much to ask. I wasn't out to hurt anybody. You have to break some eggs to make an omelette."

Yes, she thought, sighing, that was Steve's philosophy of life in a nutshell. He was driven to succeed. It was in his bones, his blood, his genes. His father had been a high-powered movie-maker, a man who'd done it all. Steve was fighting his way out from under a formidable shadow.

"Has this messed up you and Gray, too?" he asked, concern evident in his voice.

Pressing palms to her stomach, Sunny prepared herself to hear what she both dreaded and needed to know. "Was Gray in on this from the first?"

Silence prevailed.

She drilled Steve with her eyes. "I want the truth, *now*. The article says he agreed to make it look like we were having a romance."

"Sunny," he groaned, "don't put me in the middle of this. Gray's in New York, call him. Or better yet, wait until he comes home—"

"You're *smack* in the middle of it, Steve," she cut in fiercely, "and you'd damn well better tell me what I want to know."

"He agreed, not at first, but he came around."

She tried to stand but her legs were shaking too much. "Why? Why did he come around?"

"I don't know. Maybe because he could see that the rumors were working, maybe because of his attraction to you."

"In that order?"

"Yeah, no—" He groaned. "I don't know, Sunny."

So Gray was under orders to romance her. Was anything he said or did the truth? She looked away, grimacing inside. Indignation bit at her jaws, and a creeping sense of humiliation worked at her self-esteem. *Get out of here,* a voice told her.

Rising unsteadily, she walked toward the door.

"Hey, where're you going?" With a racking cough, Steve pushed himself up to a sitting position. "Sunny, you're not going to get difficult about this, are you? Who cares why Gray did it? He's madly in love with you now."

She hesitated, hated herself for asking. "Did he tell you that?"

"Well," he hedged, "not in so many words, but anyone could see..."

He'd never told her that in so many words either. "What's not to love" was *not* "I love you." A swell of insecurity broke like a wave inside her. All of Gray's evasive behavior came rushing back. Along with her own foolish eagerness to excuse him. Why hadn't she insisted he open up about his past?

"Listen," Steve said desperately, "I know this is a lousy way for you to find out, but don't let it get you crazy, okay? It's show biz, Sunny."

"Yeah," she echoed. "Show biz." Gray was a performer—a damn good act on camera. And in private, too...?

Steve threw back the covers and tried to get out of bed. "I know what you need," he cajoled. "You need to get away from here for a few days. I've got a house in Benedict Canyon. You'll go there, you'll rest, lie in the sun, get some perspective on this situation."

His patronizing tone triggered a flash of anger. Who did he think he was dealing with? An idiot child? Was that their attitude all along, his and Gray's? That Sunny couldn't be told? That Sunny couldn't handle it?

"Why you . . . bastard," she said, whirling around.

Steve's eyes widened. He clutched his stomach and tee-tered toward the bathroom. "Now look what you've done," he accused. "I think I'm going to be—"

"Sick?" she snapped. "Good, you deserve to be sick, you—you fink! You deserve to waste away with a horrible, incurable affliction."

As he lunged for the commode, she muttered an oath and strode from the room. Arms folded, she marched to the door—and realized she had no car. She could call a taxi, or walk. In this dress? She retreated in a huff to a wooden deck overlooking the harbor.

The lights dancing across the water merged in an angry blur as she leaned into the railing, arms still tightly crossed. How many people were in on it? she wondered. The pro-duction staff, the entire crew, maybe? The whole country knows by now, she thought bitterly, remembering the arti-cle. Nothing like being a coast-to-coast buffoon.

Her mind darted back to that first night in Hawaii. The way she'd broken through her paralyzing fears, run to Gray's room like a crazy woman, soaking wet. She could never had risked such lunatic behavior for any other man . . . *could never have risked such ecstasy*.

How many times since they'd first met had he accurately read her fears, her secret needs? Had he used her weak-nesses to manipulate her? A sudden sharp pain robbed her of breath. She pulled her arms free, clenched her fists. Oh God, if even a tiny portion of his motivation for becoming involved with her had been to promote the show, then she hated him. *Hated him desperately*.

She fell against the railing and dropped her head into her curled hands. With a quick breath, she tried to hold back the chaotic geyser of emotion building inside her.

Several minutes passed before the intimate laughter of a passing couple coaxed her back. She lifted her head in time to see their rapt gazes and shiny smiles. The man draped an arm about the woman's shoulders, brought her around to meet his laughing eyes. They quieted then, their smiles fading, their features engaging in a miraculous transformation from joy to such naked longing that Sunny had to look away.

Pain locked in her throat, so much pain she couldn't swallow, couldn't hold back the tears that stung at her eyelids. An aching memory nudged her heart. She and Gray had shared themselves like that. Those feelings couldn't be fabricated, could they? They had to be mutual. They had to be real.

Blinking away the tears, she stared out at the water's gentle tidal movement. She might not know much about him, but he wasn't cruel. He wasn't the kind of man who would use a woman's love as a weapon against her.

She heard Steve's shuffling footsteps behind her. "I'm sorry, Sunshine," he said, his voice unsteady.

She turned around and looked into eyes as sad and remorseful as a penitent child's. His face was long and drawn, ghostly pale.

"I'm an ass," he said, sighing, his shoulders hunched. "An ass and a screw up. So what else is new?"

He looked so pathetic, she heaved a sigh, a sucker for a pair of sad eyes. "You're darn right you are," she said, nodding. "And short of a miracle, you probably always will be."

"No probably about it." He managed a wobbly grin.

She tried to return it, but her mouth began to quiver, catching in a trembling arc. Tears filled her eyes. "Oh, Steve," she whispered suddenly, abruptly. "I love him."

His eyes narrowed, flinched as though he could feel the wave of emotion moving through her. "I know, Sunshine, I know."

He held out his arms, and she walked slowly to him. Sighing out a tight sob, she laid her head against his chest. Tears rolled down her cheeks.

"I want you to get away from here for a while," he said, holding her, rocking her. "And I'm not taking no for an answer. I'll talk to Gray—"

She shook her head, wiping away tears. "No...no, I have to talk to him myself." Sighing, she shrugged out of his arms, took a deep breath and hitched up her dress.

"Hey, where're you going?" he called after her as she stalwartly headed for his office.

"To call Gray in New York."

"You can do that later," he insisted, hobbling after her. "When you're less emotional. You'll be more objective."

She paused at his office doorway. "Please," she said, between sniffles. "I need to be alone now, okay?" Shutting the door behind her, she leaned against it, staring at the telephone.

She had to hear the truth from Gray, even if it killed her. And she had to hear it now. Settling herself into Steve's leather executive chair, she clutched the phone in her lap and began to tap out the numbers of Gray's hotel.

A brusque switchboard operator put her through to Gray's room. Each ring vibrated through Sunny's brittle nerves. After ten, she exhaled a tense expletive.

The office door burst open. "What's wrong?"

"Nothing," she said, clutching the phone to her ear, waving Steve out of the office. "He's not answering."

"Okay, so he's not in his room, so you'll call him later, in a couple of days—"

She winced as another ring shrilled in her ear. "I'll damn sure keep calling until I get him," she said grimly, hanging up the phone. "Now get out of here."

An hour of building tension passed. With each aborted call, her nerves grew so taut they nearly snapped when someone finally picked up the phone.

"Hello?" a woman's voice bubbled.

Sunny's heart sank. She had the wrong room. "Nothing, never mind," she mumbled. "I was calling room 420."

"You have 420," the woman said breathlessly. "If you're calling Gray, I'll have to have him call you back. He's in the shower now..." The words trailed off with a suggestion of laughter.

A snap of anxiety brought Sunny upright. "Who is this?"

"I beg your pardon?"

Hands shaking, Sunny told herself to hang up the phone. "Who are you?" she asked. "What's your name?"

"I really don't think—who's calling?"

"Kristin?" Sunny whispered. "Is this Kristin?"

A tense pause. "How did you know?"

Eleven

Oblivious to the orange-splashed twilight sky, Sunny walked down the driveway of Steve's small hideaway home in Benedict Canyon. She reached the narrow tree-lined road and began to follow its winding descent to God only knew where, because she certainly didn't.

Had she only been here two days? It seemed like two years. Her thoughts slipped back to the moment she'd come out of Steve's office numb with shock. "Whatever it is," he'd pleaded, "don't fly off the handle. We'll work it out." He'd immediately arranged to have her driven to this lush, essentially undeveloped canyon where Hollywood movers and shakers escaped from fast-lane stress.

Sunny interrupted her shuffling steps long enough to fish a Snickers bar—the only thing that helped in moments of complete despair—from her jeans and break open the wrapper.

Steve had promised the canyon's fertile green tranquility would ease her turmoil. Instead, the isolation had given her exactly what she didn't need. Time. Time to torture herself replaying the telephone call and imagining vivid scenarios of Gray and Kristin.

A sigh forced itself out. Life hurt; life didn't play fair.

Well…what did you expect? *happily ever after?* she asked herself, listlessly nibbling the peanuts out of their caramel encasement. Did you really think you were going to exchange a fifteen-year commitment for a quicky, add-water-and stir romance and come out of it with your heart intact? Instant love inevitably lead to instant disenchantment, didn't it?

She rounded a bend in the narrow road. What bothered her most was the dull, aching web that held her somewhere between heartbreak and hatred. She'd cursed him, cried over him and now she wanted desperately to hate him. Forever. But she couldn't. She didn't even know what he'd *done*.

Exhaling a soft moan, she wondered if she'd ever be ready to know. There were too many harrowing possibilities, and the thought that any one of them might be true made her want to curl up and die inside.

Oh yes, ignorance seemed the wiser condition.

She kicked at a pebble and missed. Gray would be back in two days. She'd have to be ready by then.

Head down, she heard the accelerating whine of an engine and looked up just in time to see a black blur swerve around the corner and come straight at her.

Animal terror locked her in place. She couldn't run, couldn't scream, *couldn't save herself.* Wrenching back with a soundless shriek, she stumbled and nearly fell.

The car roared at her, ripped through the roadside gravel and wheeled around hard, missing her by inches.

Rigid with fear, she stared down at the gleaming black fender vibrating near her legs. Heat blasted her face as the engine revved and died. A horrible quivering weakness crawled up her legs, grasped at her stomach. Dizzying static flashed inside her head.

I'm going to faint, she realized. The candy bar slipped from her fingers as she crumpled to her knees, then dizzily slid to the ground and lay there, waiting for the world to blink out like a light bulb.

It never did. Her vision swimming, she saw a huge dark panel opening over her and vaguely recognized it as the car door. A familiar voice bathed the sound waves that bombarded her ears. "Gray?" she breathed weakly, trying to bring the face above her into focus. His deep, resonant laughter rippled across the chords of her memory. "Gray? Is that you?"

A dark beard materialized first, then brown eyes and eyebrows slanted with concern.

When had Gray grown a beard? Suddenly the sum total of the parts congealed into a whole, and Sunny realized she was looking into the worried face of Neil Butler... and hearing the sonorous voice of Graham Chance.

I'm in shock, she decided instantly.

"Did I hit you? Are you all right?" Neil asked.

He pushed the car door open wider and carefully stepped over her body. Kneeling, he had the three top buttons undone on her blouse before she summoned up enough strength to push his hand away and croak, "Stop it, I'm fine."

"Are you sure?" he asked, helping her sit up.

She made a wobbly attempt to get to her feet, and with his help, finally made it.

"Just curious," he said, stabilizing her with a hand on her arm, "but why were you standing in the middle of my driveway?"

"Was I?" She looked down, saw that the asphalt drive beneath her feet stretched through the trees to a sprawling wood-shingled house. The familiar sound of male laughter made her jump. All her senses pricked to life. That *was* Gray's laugh. "What the heck . . . ?"

"The car radio," Neil explained, correctly interpreting her confusion.

"Of course," she breathed, leaning against the black Rolls. At this very moment, Gray's voice was entertaining radio owners all over the country.

"Would that my larynx had that affect on women," Neil complained good-naturedly.

She listened long enough to realize Gray was interviewing a Tony Award-winning Broadway actress and then reached inside and switched the program off. "No you don't," she muttered. "It's a curse in disguise."

"You'd know," he said sympathetically. "Get in, I'll drive you up to the house and feed you some VSOP cognac I keep for medicinal purposes."

They reached his front door without further incident. Neil gallantly helped her inside, left the door hanging wide open and guided her to a room-spanning sectional couch. Once he had her settled, he poured them both a balloon glass of Courvoisier.

"I heard we left Randolph Grant's party too soon," he said, coming to sit next to her. "Somebody locked Madeline Downs in the john. Turns out she's claustrophobic."

Sunny stifled a groan and took a large swallow of her cognac. "Oh God, no—really?"

"Yeah," Neil said, chuckling. "By the time they got her out of there, she was really wigged out. Her fashion designer friend tried to slap some sense into her—gently, mind you—"

Sunny took another swallow, choked and began to giggle. Blame it on the cognac—or on nearly being run down by an anarchist director, conned by her producer, *thrown over by her lover.* Heck, blame it on the smog. Whatever the reason, she felt the giggles bubbling up like ginger ale.

"S-slapped some s-sense?" she spluttered. "Oh God, what did Madeline do?"

Neil began to laugh, too. "She messed up his designer tux pretty bad, sprained his neck—"

The brandy in Sunny's mouth spewed out in a fine spray. "Sp-sprained his neck!" She grabbed for Neil's arm, missed and fell against his shoulder, laughing. "How? *How?*"

"Rumor says that she had him in a half nelson—"

They both lost control then, Sunny helplessly hanging on to Neil to keep from rolling onto the floor. Neil tried to wrest the brandy from her hand before she spilled it.

As they rolled and clutched, a low-spoken comment came from behind, slicing through their waves of laughter. "I see I'm interrupting something."

That voice again. A frisson of recognition moved up Sunny's spine, electrifying every muscle fiber.

"Chance?" Neil said, turning first.

"You're supposed to be in New York," Sunny blurted all at once, her back still to him.

"I'm rarely where I'm supposed to be," he said quietly. "And neither are you. Steve said you'd be at his place."

"But I heard you—the radio—"

"You've heard of taped interviews?"

Realizing she had a death grip on Neil's arm, Sunny quickly let go. With trembling fingers, she set her cognac on a glass cocktail table and stood up.

She turned, saw Gray's icy blue eyes flicker over her and felt her stomach go hollow. Was her blouse still unbuttoned? Glancing down, she had her answer. A gaping neckline, wrinkled, dirt-smudged clothing...total dishevelment.

"You're coming with me," Gray said, moving toward her.

"No," she breathed instinctively, backing up.

"Hey, man," Neil said, holding up his arms. "If the lady doesn't want to go..."

"If you ever want to direct another picture," Gray muttered, "stay out of this."

The director shrugged, dropped his arms and backed toward the nearest doorway. "Never let it be said that I stood in the path of true love." Smiling, he saluted and disappeared.

Gray's eyes targeted Sunny again. "We can do this easy, or we can do it hard, but one way or another, you're coming with me."

Her heart thundered as he reached her in a few lithe strides.

Flinching from his grasp, she snapped, "All right, all right, I'll come with you." He made no attempt to stop her as she moved ahead of him and marched out the still-open front door.

His red Alfa Romeo waited in the driveway. "How did you know I was here?" she asked.

"You dropped your Snickers bar in the road," he muttered. "Who the hell else eats the peanuts first?"

Was there a smile behind that dark growl? "Most of the world's greatest thinkers," she retorted, balking as he opened the car door and waved her in. "Listen here, Chance," she said severely. "This may seem like great macho fun to you, but there's a word for dragging people around against their will."

"Kidnapping?" he said, catching her wrist, pulling her to him. His pupils shrank to minute specks of fury. "And is there a word for a woman caught redhanded with a man she barely knows?" His finger drew an accusing path down the neckline of her blouse and held the material open.

"You—!" she gasped, trying to wrench away. "You—in New York, with *her* in your room—and you're accusing me of being caught red—"

"New York can wait," he cut in, tightening his claim on her wrist. "Right now I want to know what's going on between you and Butler. Get in the car."

The sheer menace in his voice sent waves of apprehension through her. The crimson horizon licked glimmering light through his hair as the sun dropped from the sky. His eyes glinted incandescent in the twilight. For one suspended moment, he was no longer Gray; he was the night devil.

The image raised a shiver along her shoulder blades.

"Get in," he repeated. She got into the car, perched stiffly in the bucket seat and wondered if she should make a run for it as he strode around to the driver's side. No, she'd be lucky to make it to the road, and a chase scene wasn't likely to improve his mood.

"There's nothing to tell about me and Butler," she insisted, stealing a cautious glance as he eased long legs beneath the wheel. She jumped as his arm brushed against her chest as he leaned over to lock the door. Tensing triceps crowded her breasts. A deep, darting sensation made her catch an extra breath.

He twisted the ignition key, and the Alfa Romeo ground out the will of its impatient owner. Gravel sprayed in a wake behind them as he turned out of the driveway.

"Where are you going?" she asked, her voice shrill. "Steve's house is the other way."

"I don't want you staying at Steve's house," he said, a muscle flexing in the angled plane of his jawline. "I'm feeling territorial tonight. You're coming to my place."

She discerned a sheer masculine need for mastery in the way he wheeled the car around the curve. This was a male in the throes of animal drives and biological imperatives. A stag cutting his chosen doe from the herd.

And she was the doe? "Listen," she advised him, "if you think this enraged male territoriality stuff is in any way appealing, think again. Civilized women prefer a more subtle approach.''

The car ground onto the shoulder of the road and jolted to a stop. Sunny gasped as he took her arm and brought her to him. ''Civilized women don't eat the peanuts out of candy bars, or wear their blouses open to the navel, *or fall all over scroungy Hollywood directors.* What were you doing? Auditioning for a part?''

Before she could even attempt an answer, his mouth found hers, moving, taking her lips with searing slowness. ''Civilized women don't act like you do in bed.''

''You bastard!'' she breathed, her hands flattening, pressing against his chest. ''I've never acted like that with anyone but you.''

A low hiss of release fanned over her face. ''Thank God for that,'' he grated, his voice roughening with an emotion that made her waver. Behind his low-pitched fury, she heard another chord. Fear. Her heart began to pound. Instantly, she realized he'd been terrified of losing her to someone else.

His thumbs pressed into her cheeks as he gathered handfuls of her hair into tight knots. ''You may be a free woman now, but I can't handle the thought of sharing you with jerks like Butler.''

His eyes burned a covert warning into her brain. Don't play games with me, woman, they seemed to say. Don't mess with my limited control.

With a groaning, pent-up exhalation, he released her all at once, his eyes raking over her, grimacing at the sight of her gaping blouse. As he turned away, she quickly buttoned it up.

He started the car, switched on the lights and roared down the hill, taking each curve as if it was the ultimate test of his skill.

''You're going too fast,'' she protested, aware of the tension that vibrated between them like a third presence in the car. He glanced at her, and she instinctively read the stark emotion in his features . . . anger, desire and something hidden beneath the others, a gripping signal that took her by storm. Pain, she saw pain in his eyes.

She felt the stirrings of sympathy, a warm rush that reached out to encompass him. Even fierce masculine pride couldn't completely hide his vulnerability. *She understood.* Seeing her with Butler had enraged him, yes, but it had cut into him, too. He felt betrayed. Betrayed. How well she knew that word. Her recent hurt welled inside her, but now, diffused by the emotion of the moment, it became a connecting link.

Hovering on the edge of touching him, she recoiled as he veered around the next curve, swearing softly. She saw headlights coming at them and screamed. As the car whirred past, she dropped her head back and exhaled "Are we still alive?"

"Relax—I know what I'm doing," he said, his voice low. "Maybe you prefer Butler's driving? I heard you left Rudolph Grant's party with him Friday night."

He knew about Grant's party? Her heart jerked. How did she explain that? "Neil drove me to Steve's," she told him, her voice unsteady, *"that's all."*

She pressed her palm against her rising chest and shut her eyes. From nowhere, a name blared at her as though someone had shouted it. *Kristin.*

"Who is Kristin?" she blurted, her eyes coming open. "What does she mean to you?"

"She's my brother's wife."

"What?" She sprang upright.

"Later," he warned.

"No—*now*." My God, what had he done? "I have to know now, Gray."

Stubbornly silent, he turned right, accelerating along a narrow hedged drive that opened onto a spectacular hacienda-style home. Stucco wings, red-tiled roofs and wrought-iron fences painted a graceful portrait of old Spain.

"Is this yours?" she asked.

The car pulled around the circular drive, stopped in front of iron gates and a courtyard entry.

Ignoring her question, he turned to her, his features taut. "If there's anything between you and Butler, tell me now." The pain she'd seen earlier was pierced with suspicion.

"And if there is?" she said, soft defiance in her voice.

He had her arm before she could jerk away. "Are you saying that you and he—?"

"I'm saying that he and I are *friends*," she countered, "nothing more."

Without another word, he let himself out, came around to her side and opened the door.

"No way. I'm not budging," she warned him. "Not until you answer a couple of my questions."

"I'm not in the mood for questions." His whisper-harsh resonance sent out ripples of unyielding authority.

She stared up at his imposing, dark-lit form and felt the flare of her own stubborn pride. "And I'm not in the mood to be made a fool of again," she said, folding her arms. "I may have bought that line once about the past being none of my business and the future being irrelevant, but I've grown up a little since Hawaii."

He began to smile. "You're a big girl now, huh?"

"Yeah," she said, chin thrusting high. "And I want a thorough account of your checkered past before I set foot in that Spanish . . . den of iniquity. And," she added, rearing out of his reach, "we're going to talk futures."

"Futures?" he said, an eyebrow lifting. "You selling commodities?"

"I'm perfectly serious."

"You're perfectly irresistible." The split-second warning his eyes flashed came too late. He pulled her out of the car, hooking one arm beneath her knees and the other around her shoulders before she'd caught her breath.

"Consider yourself kidnapped," he said, kicking the car door shut.

"Consider yourself with two broken ribs," she gritted, squirming in his tight hold. She dug an elbow into his chest.

Exhaling a curse, he doubled over and nearly unloaded her onto the driveway. Another expletive singed her ears as he fought to catch his balance, his grip crushing the wind out of her.

The iron gate banged open. She bounced breathlessly in his grip for a few strides before the door to the house swung wide and she was in a skylighted foyer.

"Put me down," she wheezed, flinching as the door crashed shut.

"With pleasure," he said, setting her upright.

It took her a moment to catch her breath, wheel around and brush some dignity back into her untidiness. Finishing, she sensed him behind her.

The alarms began inside her as his body brushed hers, signaling its impending threat like the coil of a snake's tail just before it strikes.

His arm slid under her breasts, pulled her back and pinned her up against the foyer wall all in one facile movement. "Didn't anybody ever tell you you're not supposed to fight your captor," he asked, his voice a low drum roll. He had the look of a man sure of himself, of his imminent victory.

Too damn sure, she decided, her heart pounding wildly. She pushed against him blindly. He retaliated by capturing her wrists and pinning them over her head with one hand.

His near smile was saturated with rogue charm. "I guess it's safe to assume no one has," he acknowledged, holding her straining limbs still with his free arm and a strategically placed leg.

"When I get loose—" she threatened.

"What?" he breathed, his eyes as ardently blue as a rain-washed sky. "What will you do?"

"Let me go and find out," she promised, a soft snarl lacing the warning.

He sobered then, easing her away from the wall, bringing her arms down gradually to imprison them behind her back. "I can't Sunny," he said, his voice hoarsening with urgent male need, "I *can't* let you go." His crooked finger nudged her chin up and his parted lips brushed their textured softness over hers in a scintillating, heart-subduing kiss.

His fire and gentleness opened her up like a soft crescendo. Moaning, she almost thought she heard music playing...bells, woodwinds, the soft rolling glissando of harp strings.

All her senses rushed to hold him as he began to ease back too soon, much too soon. "There," he said, running his finger over the glowing lips he'd just kissed. "Can you honestly tell me that you aren't glad to be here, and maybe—" he let the word linger, seemingly forever "—just a little turned on?"

If that self-satisfied smile hadn't appeared, she might have conceded the question. But it had appeared. And it riled her. "Cool as a cucumber," she lied.

"Oh, Sunny," he murmured with a low rich chuckle. "Haven't we played this scene before? I know this body, remember?" he said, running his knuckles over the pulse of her throat. "I know what it needs, what makes it...hum."

Her narrowing glare only seemed to encourage him.

"If I were to undo this blouse," he said, fingering the top button, "I'd find breasts budded, aching to be touched...wouldn't I?"

She stared rebelliously into his eyes, so aware that her body was betraying her, that a sharp inner tremor made his words true. A soft gasp quivered in her throat as her blouse fell open and he slipped his hand inside. Her breasts came alive with sweet aching need under the enveloping warmth of his fingers, the pressure of his palms.

A low moan rumbled in his chest. "Wouldn't I?" he said, his voice catching with an emotion he couldn't control. "And if I were to ease down these jeans, I'd feel your stomach muscles drawing tight, painfully tight, and your thighs tingling—" His fingers worked her waistband snap loose.

She caught at his hand. "My thighs are completely indifferent," she insisted, her voice weakened by a spasming thrill as his fingers rode down with the zipper. *She was talking a better game than she was playing*.

He groaned softly, shook his head. Catching her by the shoulders, he gave her a long impassioned stare. His features contracted with need as he curled his fingers into her hair. "You're bluffing, Sunny, your eyes are giving you away." His breath rustled around her like a hot gust of wind. "Pleasure makes pupils dilate, and yours are black with passion."

The same passion darkened his eyes, and the force of it reduced her protest to an unintelligible murmur. A magnetic pull induced her to sway forward imperceptibly, to lean into him. Their bodies brushed with light breathless pressure. A surge of excitement left her weakened as his mouth neared hers, and she felt herself responding helplessly to the primal scent of aroused masculinity, to the aura of waiting, caged-in heat.

His hands coiled tight, pulling her to him, the kiss deepening, sweeping her along with its dark rushing momentum, buffeting her senses into dazed submission. She heard him mutter something low and grindingly sensual, unbearably exciting. A flush climbed her body, escalating like a dangerously high fever.

She felt his hands rushing down over her breasts, her rib cage and stealing under the waistband of her jeans to grip her hipbones and bring her up against his fire. The pressure of his fingers awakened primitive desires. "And if I touched you here," he murmured, his voice hoarse as his thumbs made small, tight circles in a breathtaking incursion toward her secrets. "I'd find a woman in throbbing need of—"

A knifelike flash of desire cut off her breath. "Yes, dammit, yes," she admitted spontaneously, a frantic hiss against his lips.

His tight release of air bathed her face. "I knew it," he said, his eyes burning into hers. As strong fingers reasserted their claim on her hips, urging her against his heat, a shock wave of stimulation moved through her body.

"Come on," he said, pulling her with him down two tiled steps and into a low-lit indoor garden. Fertile green scents mingled with the heavy fragrance of lilac and jasmine. A cushioned deck stretched next to a rock grotto stocked with goldfish.

Sunny stood, trembling in the glimmering light, her breath suspended as Gray's fingers worked impatiently to remove the rest of her clothing.

As her clothes dropped to the floor around her, his hands on her bare skin brought her to a quick, gasping state of heightened pleasure. Excitement rocked through her.

"Let me touch you now," she breathed, catching his hands. Their eyes met with an intense burst of light.

He pulled his sweater over his head and tossed it aside. His nostrils flared with a sudden harsh breath as she worked his slacks free and caressed him to agonizing tautness.

With a harsh moan, he caught her hand, and a current connected them, racing through them like chain lightning.

"I want you," she said urgently, pulling him down with her, bringing him into the valley of her thighs.

Their naked skin touched with a thunderbolt of sensation.

Their bodies were the lightning in a storm-dark sky, two raw wires of light, connecting, spraying sparks, exploding with the passion of raw, uncurbed energy.

She felt searing wrenches of pleasure as he alternately eased and forced his way full into her. He was a twisting laser of electricity entering her body, searching, invading, penetrating the fabric of her soul.

Quick-striking, passion took them to turbulent heights. Sheened with sweat, they became the storm's center, gasping, writhing in a brilliant and cataclysmic joining of flesh and spirit.

The final throes of release brought piercing pleasure and the shuddering mindlessness of perfection.

In the aftermath, Sunny held fast to Gray, her body still shivering through a series of tiny, slow-motion explosions like glistening raindrops hitting a leaf and bursting in all directions.

Long afterward, limbs still inextricably tangled, they drowsed languidly. A smile of contentment warmed Sunny's lips as she snuggled deeper, luxuriating in the warmth of his possessive embrace.

Half-hoping to wake him, she blew a soft stream of air through his chest hair, watching it quiver and spring back into soft golden curls. When he didn't even stir, she settled back to muse on the vagaries of life.

Her smile faded a little as an unpleasant possibility intruded on her blissful state. Had all of Gray's wonderful possessive passion been nothing more than a macho reaction to finding her with another man?

And what about his part in the romance hype? *Sunny Tyler isn't my type, but I'll play along?*

And that offhand remark about his brother's wife?

She pushed up, stared narrow-eyed at his face, his expression so little-boy innocent while he slept. This overgrown bully had coerced her into a passionate interlude without so much as a word of explanation.

"Gray—wake up," she said, shaking him.

"Hmm...Kristin?" he mumbled, slinging an arm languorously above his head, as though drifting in a pleasant dreamworld.

Twelve

Fury bit at Sunny's trembling lips. *Kristin?* How dared he dream about her. "Okay—" she jabbed at his exposed ribs "—let's hear about Kristin!"

"Hey!" he grunted, bringing his arm down protectively. He met her glare, a tinge of mischief lurking beneath the blue of his eyes.

Staring down her nose at him, deeply suspicious, she realized he hadn't been dreaming about Kristin, *hadn't even been asleep!* Relief mixed with her outrage. Was that a wink, she wondered as he grinned up at her, or was he developing his own nervous twitch?

"Gotcha," he said, his lips quivering with suppressed laughter.

"What?" she said, a low growl of outrage. "How can you joke about something like that? If I were the violent type, you'd be begging for mercy now."

"And if I were the violent type, you and Butler would have been in deep trouble about an hour ago," he reminded her, golden eyebrows twitching. "I might have been persuaded to spare you, though."

"Don't distract me with compassion," she snapped. "You and Kristin are—"

"What?" He cocked his head, waiting.

"Clandestine lovers?" She threw up her hands in frustration. "I don't know. What are you?"

"Is that what you think?" He lifted himself up, and propped his head on an elbow, a pose that made him look disconcertingly like he was auditioning for centerfold work. His blue eyes flickered. "You want the whole truth?"

Her eyes narrowed. "You bet I do!"

"Care to try coaxing it out of me?" He dodged her murderous lunge. Rolling off, he sprang to his feet, all agile grace, and grabbed for his slacks. "I'm sorry," he said quickly, grinning, hopping sideways as he tried to get into his pants. "It's just this terrific mood I'm in."

Terrific mood? She, who hadn't enough killer instinct to set out ant traps, felt murder flowing in her veins. *I'd sell my mother for a bat to brain him with!* She jerked to her feet, felt a breeze and looked down. *You're naked, Sunny. Naked people don't commit murder!*

His guilty cough reclaimed her attention. Hastily, she knelt and picked up her clothes.

"Hey—I'm sorry," he tried again, having the good sense to sound sincere this time.

Seeing the mute appeal in his blue eyes, she felt an uncontrollable warmth soften her violence-bent heart. The forgive-me-or-I-may-not-live message in his features nearly made her sigh aloud. And then he winked, so engagingly that the warmth swelled again—*and dropped lower.* Oh no! He wasn't going to foul her brain waves with passion again! "Not a chance, Chance," she resolved aloud.

Ignoring his momentary bafflement, she began to dress. "Do you mind?" she asked pointedly, signaling him to turn around.

He shrugged and complied. "I could help," he suggested matter-of-factly. "Four hands are faster than two."

Ignoring him, she hurriedly shivered into her clothing. By the time she'd finished he was sitting on the steps. She leveled a point-blank stare at him. "Talk."

"It's not what you think, Sunny," he said quietly. His eyes held hers until her heart began to beat erratically.

"I'll be the judge of that. Stop stalling."

"Okay." He grimaced, squirming a little on the step. She had a quick impression of a counseling client about to confess something he wasn't very proud of. Did that make her the counselor? What a refreshing reversal. Go ahead, squirm fella, she thought heartlessly.

He cleared his throat. "Let's see," he began, exhaling. "I met Kristin for the first time at one of Mark's, my brother's, tennis tournaments. He shocked the hell out of me by introducing her as his fiancée. She was a pretty, vivacious girl, full of eager questions about my radio psychology work—"

His jaw jutted in hesitation. "I don't know why I didn't see what was happening. She started visiting my office, my clinical practice, said she was thinking about going into the field." He lifted a shoulder. "There was no reason not to believe her."

Sunny felt his conflict, saw his chest move with a long exchange of air. "Kristin had stars in her eyes," he said finally, quietly. "Maybe I didn't see the situation for what it was because I wanted to believe there was nothing to it—just a mild case of hero worship, a passing phase."

He shook his head. "Now I realize she'd built me up in her mind as some kind of celebrity; she'd even sung my praises to Mark. That must have devastated him. He'd al-

ways felt diminished by his 'big brother's' achievements—''
Gray's short laugh was colored with pain. "All those years
of clinical training and I couldn't allay my own kid brother's
resentment toward me."

After a stretch of silence, a hoarseness crept into his voice.
"Mark came to my place one night, drunk, accused me of
trying to take her away from him, insisted Kristin was in love
with me, not him. God, he was hurt."

He shifted physically, and Sunny could almost see the
painful memory move through him. "I tried, but I couldn't
convince him that I hadn't encouraged her, couldn't make
him understand that her infatuation wasn't love." He shook
his head. "Anyway, that was the beginning of the end."

"They broke up?" she asked, hushed.

He nodded. "A three-way split. Kristin and Mark called
off their engagement, and I didn't hear from my younger
brother for two years." His jaw flexed.

After a moment, he looked up at her. "They got back together a few months ago, but Mark still refused to see me.
That note you misunderstood was Kristin's attempt to patch
things up. She'd planned an accidental meeting between
Mark and I, thinking we'd talk it out, make up—" Expel-
ling a sad, self-mocking laugh, he looked up at Sunny. "You
weren't the only one who misunderstood the note's meaning. I never answered her."

"Oh Gray," she said, trying to keep the reproach from
her voice. "Why didn't you tell me?"

Exhaling, he settled back as though to shed the emotional burden he'd been carrying. "I almost did a couple of
times, but I just couldn't take the risk. If that story ever hit
the scandal sheets, Mark's life, and Kristin's, would be sheer
hell. I'd done them enough damage without inflicting the
paparazzi on them."

"And you—" She hesitated, eyebrows furrowing. "You
thought I couldn't be trusted to know?"

Steepling his fingers, he touched his lips to cover a flicker of amusement. "You're not exactly the soul of discretion."

"Oh?"

"Correct me if I'm wrong," he said, unable to subdue a grin, "but wasn't it you who spilled the beans in front of cast, crew, God and everybody? Does 'Ted and I are through' ring a bell?"

The twinkle in his blue eyes nearly melted her indignation. "One slip and I'm branded a big mouth?"

"Don't be angry, Sunny," he coaxed, persuasive, sobering. "It wasn't just you. This was a personal issue, deeply personal. I had to work it through before I could talk about it. I wasn't ready then."

He looked so intent, so sincere, she almost forgot the crucial question. "Kristin? She was in your room. Why?"

A flaxen eyebrow slanted. Suddenly, he was grinning again. "God, but you're irresistible when you're on the offensive. Come here," he said, crooking a finger. "Come here and I'll tell you anything you want to know."

She almost went. A soft shudder traveled her spine. "Uh-uh . . . answers first."

He sat forward. "Well, I was not, as you've apparently assumed, entertaining Kristin alone in my room. She'd finally convinced Mark that I wasn't the competitive, ego-maniacal big brother he thought I was, and the two of them showed up at my hotel room, married." He shifted, a catch husking his voice. "I don't think I've ever been so glad to see anyone as I was that stubborn brother of mine."

"He comes by it naturally," Sunny observed, her voice softening with emotion. "Stubbornness, I mean."

Gray beckoned again. "Come here, *I need you*."

She joined him then, shivering, tucking her head into the hollow of his shoulder and burrowing close for several blissful seconds. "I'm glad about your brother," she told him, realizing even as she said it that there was no need; he knew.

Soothed by the steady thud of his heart, the warmth of his body, she basked in the awareness of how right it felt to be with him. The quiet intimacy freed her to ask a question that had been in the back of her mind since their afternoon of "margaritas and honesty" in that dark little bar. "Gray," she said very softly, still snuggled close to him, "you told me once that I was a classic case of something—"

She felt his chest jerk. Was he chuckling? She angled her head around and gave him the business with her huge hazel eyes. "Tell me, Counselor, exactly what am I a classic case of?"

He kissed her nose. "That's a beautiful preposition you just dangled."

This guy was a virtuoso at dodging the question. Nice try, Chance, she warned nonverbally, her eyes narrowing to death-ray slits.

"Okay, okay," he relented, kissing her nose again. "In the jargon of popular psychology, you were a 'best little girl in the world' if I ever saw one. You hid behind that great big smile of yours, denying your own needs in order to live up to everyone else's expectations. You were turning yourself inside out, Sunny, trying to please your parents, Ted, Steve, even your viewers."

Hmm, that wasn't such a revelation. She'd been expecting something more dramatic like delusions of grandeur or incipient paranoia. "And . . . ? What am I now?"

His smile was sudden and awesome. "Now there isn't a category that could hold you. Now you're...magnificent." He slid his fingers along her neck, brushing his thumb the length of her jawline in a warm, vibrant caress. "Believe me, there aren't many of us with the courage to face down our fears, to risk changing the course of our lives. You, lady, are as brave as they come."

His gaze bathed her in reverence, then gradually, subtly changed. "God," he breathed, "the times I wanted you—"

He broke off, exhaled deeply, shook off the feeling. "But you were off limits and nobody knew it better than I did. Even after you and Ted split, I knew you needed the freedom to find yourself, to make your own choices." He laughed softly. "Quite a challenge for a possessive guy like me."

His smile was ironic, concerned. He wanted her to understand. "You know, don't you, that if I'd won you with declarations of love and commitment, you'd simply have been exchanging Ted for me, one sure thing for another. It scared the hell out of me, Sunny, but I had to take the risk of letting you choose *me*, not what I could offer you."

Insight filled her like a soft white light. All his superhuman restraint had been for her sake. The way he'd held back after their trip to Las Vegas, and again that night in Hawaii—he'd been trying not to crowd her. He'd even risked losing her. No one but *no one* in her life had ever cared that much. Tears filled her eyes and she had to look away.

He gently caught her to him, running his hands into her hair, pressing her damp cheek against the protective hollow of his throat. A soft sob caught in her throat, releasing with such poignancy she trembled, and felt his body shudder in response. She loved this man, she did.

They grew silent then, closer than words, closer than they'd ever been. And gradually another kind of communication began . . . in the meshing of their respiration, in the slowing of his heartbeat to hers. Harmony. Simplicity. One accord. This must be perfection, she mused, or the closest I'll ever come to knowing it.

A sigh built, spilled out, rustling the quiet. She shut her eyes, drifting, warm and wondrously content . . . until another memory began to tug at her . . .

"Go away," she murmured, serenely ignoring the vague images forming in her mind...nonchalantly discounting the blurry newsprint floating through her consciousness...the article, the headline. Headline?

Oh brother. Reluctant to bring it up, to ruin the bliss, she mumbled into his chest, "Gray? About those scandal sheets—you didn't really tell that anonymous source that I wasn't your type, but you'd play along? Did you?"

When he didn't answer her head popped up. "Oh, my God. You didn't, *did you?*"

Sandy hair fell in rebellious waves across his forehead. His eyes sparkled and danced. "Does it matter?" he asked, hitching her closer. "You're definitely my type now."

He'd done it again! Finessed the question. She knew she should pursue it, sweat the truth out of him, but her heart, her foolish heart, was on his side. It swore he could never have done anything so despicable. And besides that, the slight parting of his lips, the gradual darkening of his eyes fascinated her. Phew, incredibly sensual. A brilliant idea came over her. "I think I might like to marry you."

Her matter-of-fact sincerity startled both of them.

"My God, I've created a monster," he said, chuckling nervously.

A flush colored her cheeks. Don't hold back, Sunny, she thought, an ironic smile bubbling. Lord, there was such heady power in taking the initiative. It also tickled her that he looked the closest to frightened she'd ever seen him.

"Not that it isn't a terrific idea," he assured her, shifting for position on the tiled steps. "But how do you think Blanchard's going to react to a merger of his two 'hottest properties'? Or the network? Or Steve, for that matter?"

He had a point. Would blessed matrimony be a ratings plus? She thought about it, letting him dangle for a while. "Maybe we've let Steve and the network and the ratings control us long enough," she murmured, inspired. She smiled into skeptical blue eyes. "Maybe we should stake our own personal claim on the future."

He shook his head, a touch of awe in his soft laughter. "You've come a long way, baby."

"Yeah," she agreed, smiling, flattered beyond reason. "But there's still miles of road ahead. Coming with me?"

Now his hesitation began to worry her. Maybe it wasn't just the instinctive male dread of monogamy. Maybe he really didn't want to. "Well," she said, the words trembling a little. "I guess it wasn't such a good idea."

She lifted his arm from her shoulder, walked over to the grotto and pondered on the advantages of being born a goldfish in this complex world.

After an endless silence, he addressed her back. "Did it ever occur to you that you might be giving up too easily?" He cleared his throat. "Or that I might have already considered the idea of getting married? Or even that I was going to ask you myself... eventually?"

A grin bubbled, quirked. This was too good to pass up. She whirled around. "Gotcha."

His eyes narrowed; he shook his head. "Oh, you dirty rat," he breathed. "Scare the hell out of a guy and then, while he's still dumbstruck, pull a guilt trip and make him think he's broken your heart." Springing up, he caught her before she could dart away. "That's emotional blackmail," he warned, pulling her into his arms. "Who'd ever be crazy enough to marry such a lowdown, ruthless woman?"

His embrace touched off warm, wonderful thrills. She was suddenly, vividly aware of him, of the heat radiating from his body, of even the slightest pressure of his fingertips.

"Is the offer still good?" he asked huskily, his mouth brushing her temple.

His voice played along the vibrant chords of her emotions. Fine-spun blond lashes drooped, suddenly shy. "Maybe."

Low laughter swirled warm rushes through her hair. "What does a guy have to do to win this heartless woman's hand?"

She felt herself blushing with inordinate pleasure. Lashes fluttered as she looked up at him. "Perhaps if he were more forthcoming with certain information..."

"Name it."

She feigned innocence. "Like whether or not he'd actually been so callous as to let it be known that a certain talk-show host *wasn't his type*?"

"He'd consider that request—for a price." His eyes darkened rapidly.

"Name it," she breathed.

Easing blond curls away from her face, he bent and lightly caressed her lips with his, a kiss that shimmered with fierce, tender passion. "This looks like the beginning of some interesting negotiations," he murmured.

Her lips parted spontaneously, surprised as he shifted back and began to unbutton her blouse. Anticipation quivered through her.

"Steve asked me to play along with the romance publicity," he explained tautly. "So I let him think I would." His eyes held hers. "But Steve didn't know that I wasn't playing. Not then, not now." His fingers hesitated on the snap of her jeans. "Marry me?"

"Maybe," she said, her heart trembling.

His eyes flashed with desire. Arm and neck muscles corded as though fighting a powerful impulse. She braced herself, waited a pulse-pounding second, sure he meant to—

His features flexed, held, then relaxed in a smile. "Umm...I know this ploy," he said, releasing her, stepping back to size her up. "She's holding out for more. How much do you want, woman?'' Blue eyes narrowed sensually. ''I swear I never said you weren't my type.''

She caught her lower lip between her teeth to subdue a sudden smile.

He lifted his arms. ''More? I'll stop talking about you in the third person. I'll even stop complaining about the way you eat Snickers bars. Enough?''

''Maybe.'' Her heart did a cartwheel as he caught her wrist and tugged her back into his arms.

''I'll love you until the day I die,'' he promised huskily, lacing his fingers through her hair. ''The day after.''

A shiny smile awakened her lips. Her mouth feathered over his in a trembling arc. ''Gotcha,'' she whispered, realizing a split-second later that he'd whispered it, too.

AMERICAN TRIBUTE

Where a man's dreams count for more than his parentage...

Look for these upcoming titles under the Special Edition American Tribute banner.

CHEROKEE FIRE
Gena Dalton #307—May 1986
It was Sabrina Dante's silver spoon that Cherokee cowboy Jarod Redfeather couldn't trust. The two lovers came from opposite worlds, but Jarod's Indian heritage taught them to overcome their differences.

NOBODY'S FOOL
Renee Roszel #313—June 1986
Everyone bet that Martin Dante and Cara Torrence would get together. But Martin wasn't putting any money down, and Cara was out to prove that she was nobody's fool.

MISTY MORNINGS, MAGIC NIGHTS
Ada Steward #319—July 1986
The last thing Carole Stockton wanted was to fall in love with another politician, especially Donnelly Wakefield. But under a blanket of secrecy, far from the campaign spotlights, their love became a powerful force.

AM-TRIB-1R

AMERICAN TRIBUTE

American Tribute titles now available:

 **Silhouette Desire**

COMING
NEXT MONTH

GREEN FIRE—Stephanie James
Was Rani's life endangered by inheriting an antique emerald ring? It
was a fake—but the man who appeared on her doorstep was
undeniably real. He claimed he was there to protect her....

DESIGNING HEART—Laurel Evans
Lighting director Stella Ridgeway was perfectly content with her
career; playwright Sam Forster was quite happy being alone. But
there was an undeniable magnetism between them that neither
could resist!

BEFORE THE WIND—Leslie Davis Guccione
Disheartened after a bad marriage, Whitney was determined to avoid
the pain of involvement again—until she met Paul. Paul helped her
regain her self-esteem, but could she learn to love once more?

WILLING SPIRIT—Erin Ross
Athena MacKay went to Scotland to reclaim Kildrurry, "haunted"
castle of her ancestors that had been stolen by the Burke clan.
Christopher Burke was no ghost—but could she give her heart to
the enemy?

THE BLOND CHAMELEON—Barbara Turner
Delancey was good at impersonating movie stars—and good at hiding
her real self from the man she loved. But Stuart was intrigued, and
insisted on finding the woman within.

CAJUN SUMMER—Maura Seger
Eight years ago, Arlette left the Louisiana bayou to pursue her own
career. That had meant leaving Julian behind. Now she was back, and
this time he wasn't going to let her go!

AVAILABLE THIS MONTH:

EYE OF THE TIGER
Diana Palmer

DECEPTIONS
Annette Broadrick

HOT PROPERTIES
Suzanne Forster

LAST YEAR'S HUNK
Marie Nicole

PENNIES IN THE FOUNTAIN
Robin Elliott

CHALLENGE THE FATES
Jo Ann Algermissen